KING BEATRICE

EVANGELINE

Lunar Ink Publishing

ISBN: 978-1-7328928-0-4

King Beatrice

Lunar Ink Publishing PO Box 40728 Austin, Tx 78704-9998
www.lunarinkpublishing.com

www.evangelinebooks.com

Printed in the United States of America

Lunar Ink Publishing

PART ONE

CHAPTER ONE

P hantasmagoria
(n.) a shifting series of phantasms, illusions, or deceptive appearances, as in a dream or as created by the imagination

YOU'LL FIND YOURSELF SURROUNDED BY THE UNLIKELIEST OF people.

The boy, Alex, thought he had heard that somewhere before.

You'll need who you least expect.

What a load of garbage. Alex glared at the television screen, or, more accurately, through the screen, past the actors, around the set, and straight to the directors and writers who oversaw the romanticization of that trash. He should have changed the channel an episode ago when he first stumbled upon the show, yet the poor boy found himself staring at the screen as if he were witnessing a car wreck.

Lilian, the gorgeous teen who was made "nerdy" by sticking on a pair of thick glasses, was too smart for her new adventurous and, as far as Alex was concerned, annoying band of misfits this character decided to call friends. It was all to get back at her parents, which seemed incredibly irrational considering Lillian apparently had a 4.0 GPA, suggesting that she had some sort of notable intelligence. But what did Alex know? He was only twelve and on his second episode.

It caused physical discomfort to the boy watching as Lillian got herself into all sorts of trouble, but he continued to follow her story, muttering *I-told-you-so*'s under his breath every twenty minutes. She should have stuck to solitude, Alex thought with an exaggerated sigh. *Look at what those idiots got you into this time . . .*

"Alex. Alex, honey?" The boy's mother, Marianne, looked down at her son and pursed her lips. She hated when he slipped into a daze, utterly oblivious to all around him as he focused so intently on the television. "Alex," Marianne repeated, and finally, he turned and faced her, his face showing a puzzled expression. "Honey, the summer is almost over."

"I know." He frowned and stared out the window. It was almost the end of summer and she wanted him to go outside, but he wished to stay inside where it was cool, quiet, and far from everyone else.

"Why don't you go outside? Find some friends? Mm?"

Friends. He almost laughed. Alex didn't want friends. What he wanted was peace and that was certainly not what he got his first year of middle school. Alex hadn't the faintest idea as to why his mother found the prospect of him attaining friends so enticing.

"The ladies from church are coming today. You can stay and have tea with us or . . ."

His eyes grew wide.

It was Sunday afternoon and the old ladies always came on Sunday at four o'clock. They smelled like stale perfume and raisins, and they never missed an opportunity to pinch his cheeks and tell him how handsome he was becoming.

"I'll go," he said quickly, turning off the television and heading for the door. He called for the dog who came gallivanting with a wide, silly grin on his face.

"Be back before dark!" his mother called, though she had no doubt that her son would be home long before then.

Grimacing, he closed the door behind him and clasped the leash onto Rex's collar. Eternally grateful, the yellow lab barked. There was nothing Rex loved more than a walk with Alex, even if it was in the blazing summer heat.

"Come on." Alex didn't have to pull very hard on the leash to get Rex to go. Alex took the same route every walk, so the dog already knew the path as well as he knew his own home. "You're more excited than I am."

Alex had never cared much for the outdoors; there were always too many people, and talkative people at that, especially whenever he dragged Rex along, and it was always too hot or too cold. But if he ever did have to go outside, Alex preferred it to be because he was walking Rex, his only friend.

They stopped at an intersection with shade where Alex took the opportunity to wipe the sweat from his forehead. To the left was the route they always took. It went into more residential housing and there was a shortcut to get home sooner should they both tire of the walk early, which Alex was already planning on taking. To the right was a way he'd never traveled. Three blocks down and the road ended at a forest. Alex had no knowledge of how deep it went, nor did he particularly care. Bugs. Bugs. And more bugs. No, thank you!

Sighing, Alex started to the left, but Rex had another idea.

Catching a scent, or perhaps eyeing a squirrel, Rex took off in the opposite direction. At first, the boy pulled and pulled hard, yet Rex didn't seem to notice or care; he was relentless. After a block of embarrassing fumbling, Alex gave up and let Rex lead. It wasn't until they stopped at the entrance to the wood that Alex finally put his foot down.

"No," Alex said deeply, or at least as deeply as a boy of twelve could.

Rex wasn't listening. In fact, he was sniffing with even more intensity than before. The lab wanted to go into the wood, just as he had wanted every day previous, but this walk was different.

This little forest in the middle of the city gave the boy the creeps. Sure, it was probably safe, Alex thought. However, it was far too foreign and a little too eerie for the boy to try. Alex took a few steps backwards, tugging Rex lightly, but the lab surged forward with urgency and strength that Alex wasn't expecting.

For a moment, the boy stood there, empty-handed, dumb-founded, and astonished by his pet's boldness. He shouted for Rex, and then screamed. Rex only looked back once, a bright grin on the dope's face. Alex couldn't tell if Rex thought it was a game or if he was just plain stupid, probably both, but one thing was certain: Alex had to go into the woods.

Murmuring to himself, he reluctantly put one foot in front of the other and called for Rex.

Nothing.

When Rex disappeared over a hill, Alex ran for the first time all summer. Half of him expected Rex to return instantly like a loyal lab should, but the other half couldn't help but imagine turning a corner and finding him . . . Alex didn't want to think of the nightmarish possibilities.

"Rex!" he shrieked again, panic seizing him.

Alex had lost track of the time long ago, and then got lost not long after that. He continued running, though he wasn't sure how long he could keep that up; he was terribly out of shape.

Nearly collapsing, Alex fell against a tree, clutching his chest and trying to breathe. The boy thought of his overbearing gym teacher yelling at him to put his hands behind his head if he was so out of breath, so he did. He didn't realize how hot it was, even in the shade, or how much he was sweating until just then. And the stupid breathing trick wasn't working.

Alex started pacing.

With each step another thought crept in, and with every arriving thought came the screaming fact that he couldn't breathe. *Oh God*, he thought, *Rex is dead.* Rex is dead, and then Alex would be dead because his mother was going to kill him.

A bark.

Alex leapt from death's clutches and scanned the area.

"Rex!"

Two barks.

Alex sprinted in the direction of the sound, trying his hardest to not give in to his body's desire to lie down and die right there.

Silence.

"Crap," Alex whispered. He slowed to a walk, and then stood completely still, impatient but listening.

Something stuck into his back.

He turned, assuming it was only a loose branch or something harmless, but moving only intensified the pain.

Trillions of thoughts raced through Alex's mind. Someone had snuck behind him without making a sound, and now he was going to be killed where no one would find him for weeks, maybe months.

He shut his eyes tight as if it would help.

Alex whimpered, "Please."

He was shoved hard and stumbled forward. The sharp and sudden sound of a laugh cracked and nearly made Alex pee, fearful that he'd be killed at the hands of some lunatic. But the laugh wasn't as Alex expected. It was a girl's laugh.

A girl, Alex thought, puzzled.

He regained his balance, opened his eyes, and looked around. There, just in front of him, standing proudly with one hand on her hip and the other hand grasping a large stick, with her chin up, a head of frizzy hair, and a smirk, stood a girl on a boulder.

"Who are—Rex!" Alex exclaimed as his lab appeared atop the boulder beside the girl. "Come on, boy!" Alex patted his leg and breathed a sigh of relief.

Rex looked up at the girl as if asking for permission, but stayed in place.

"*She* is not a *he,*" the girl corrected.

"*He* is my dog. Come here!" Alex whistled, but Rex obeyed the girl . . . again.

"Her name is Regenald."

"That isn't even a girl's name!"

"Well, she likes it, and that's all the matters."

Alex started to get the feeling that arguing with her was a waste of time. "Rex, we're going home. Now."

Rex headed for his owner, but the girl's grasp and petting was far more exciting. "I have an idea." She grinned and scratched Rex behind the ears. "I'll call you Regenald Rex. I think I like that much better!"

You've got to be joking, Alex thought, absolutely baffled.

"Do you want to play?" she asked after a painfully long stretch of silence.

Play? Alex didn't know if she honestly believed that keeping his dog hostage would make him want to play with her, but the girl was dead serious.

This boy was the first kid she had ever seen in that wood without a parent—he was one of the few people she had seen there at all—and to make it even better, he had a dog. He would be the perfect friend.

"I have a game that I—"

"No, thanks. Rex, come." This time the lab listened.

She watched, a smirk creeping upon her lips, as Alex looked around him, lost. Jumping down from the boulder and driving the stick into her belt loop as a sword into a sheath, the girl spoke. "Do you know how to get back?" She skipped around him theatrically.

"Yes."

"Are you sure? This place is surprisingly big and—"

"Just leave me alone." His words came out sharp and cold, and her pain and embarrassment shone clear to him. For a moment, he felt guilty. "P-please. And thank you for taking care of my dog."

Standing perfectly still and erect, the strange girl nodded to him.

He found himself somewhat astonished that she said nothing. *Better not push my luck*, Alex thought, grabbing hold of Rex's leash and hurrying off.

A few minutes later, Alex was lost. There were no people to ask for directions, no signs, not even a path to follow.

"Way to go, Rex." By that time, Alex should have been back home, both he and his furry friend rehydrating and hiding from the old church ladies up in his room and watching his favorite engineering show. "We are so lost."

The girl barged past Alex, sweeping the leash from his grasp and taking a sharp left turn. "This way," she sang, glad that she had decided to follow behind.

Submissive, Alex bowed his head and followed. He just wanted to go home. The boy glanced down at his watch. It was gone. With his luck, of course it had fallen off. Would he be hit by a bus on the way back, too?

"Stay close," the girl said to Rex just as she set him free.

"I-I really don't think it's such a good idea to let him off the leash."

"She's fine. She can be trusted."

If Rex was fine and could be trusted, thought Alex, then why was he in the forest instead of at home?

"Regenald Rex is my trusty wolf companion," she explained, slowing her speed to match Alex's.

"Wolf companion?" *She's kidding*, he thought. *Right? She can't be serious.*

"Yup! And I'm King Beatrice." She halted and pressed a hand to his chest, stopping him, too. The girl looked around, suspicious of their surroundings. Finally, she said in a hushed tone, "But be careful who you tell that to. It isn't safe to be blurting that kind of information to just anyone, you know?"

Of course, it wasn't safe. That's the kind of talk that gets you put in the looney bin!

Alex didn't know how to respond. He just stood there and stared at her. *She thinks she's a king?* He couldn't believe it. Had he done something wrong? Was he rude to his mother? Did he forget to help Dad? Alex couldn't figure out what it was that he had done to deserve the day he had had.

She wasn't surprised by the look on his face; most people expect kings to be much larger. She'd be tall one day, though, and then she'd really fit the bill.

"So . . . your name is Beatrice?"

She squinted for a moment, and then smiled and continued the trek. "It's *King* Beatrice to you."

He wouldn't be caught dead calling her king anything.

"And your name?" She petted Rex who appeared at her side.

"Alex."

Beatrice frowned, "I don't like it."

"I-It's my name."

Suddenly, she planted herself in front of him and studied the boy from head to toe. Alex felt unmeasurable levels of discomfort. No one had ever looked at him that closely before, not even when he had peed his pants in the cafeteria in the fifth grade after he asked out his crush, Pam Truly. He hated Pam Truly after that day, her and all her friends.

Beatrice had never had so much trouble coming up with a new name before. Names came so easily to her, but he stumped Beatrice.

He was scrawny, a little shorter than her, and it looked like he had never smiled in his whole life. "You seem to be a bit snotty and most definitely serious, so we'll call you . . ." she tapped her chin, "Ah! We'll call you Mr. Holberry!"

"Mr. What?" Alex didn't know just what he heard, but he knew he wasn't going to like it.

"Mr. Holberry."

"Please, my name is Alex."

"Right this way, Mr. Holberry! Now, I must warn you that we are in quite a dangerous part of my kingdom."

She was ignoring him. She had to be, thought Alex, and she had to be crazy, indisputably insane. He didn't want any part of her game. Besides, they were far too old to still play pretend. Alex, again, simply wanted out of the stupid woods.

The boy had no idea how deep in they were until Beatrice started talking, and then she kept talking and they still hadn't gotten out. Alex partly believed she was tricking him and keeping him captive in that godforsaken place as her little play toy for all of eternity.

She told him everything. She told him about the castle, the great river that led into the ocean, the cliff that overlooked the same ocean, the mountains, and the Dark Woods. Beatrice shed some knowledge, not wanting to overload the boy, about how she planned to renovate her castle, that there was a boat festival coming up, and a little about her subjects, one of which he was now considered. Beatrice had been waiting so long to share her world with someone.

"Shush! Be quiet," she warned Alex, calling Rex beside her and crouching behind a bush. "Come on, get down!" Beatrice waved him over quickly.

He didn't move. The boy didn't see anyone or anything. There were just trees and dirt and bugs and sweat and that was it. "I really just want to go home," Alex groaned, more tired than he'd ever been in his life.

Beatrice frowned and pulled him down with more force than Alex knew a girl had. "Do you see them?"

No, of course he did not see anybody. For a second, he was gullible enough to look, but they were alone. They had been the entire time.

"There are the bandits! The ones I told you about!"

A word stood out clearly to the boy as he gaped at her. Phantasmagoria. He had read it in a book once and had never thought of it again until the girl who stood before him began rambling about bandits. She suffered from that disease, that phantasmagoria. He would have bet his allowance on it.

"They're horrible," she continued, either oblivious to or not caring about how unhappy Alex was. "They've stolen nearly everything from the village just outside the Dark

Woods," she noted his confused expression, "which is where we are now."

He looked at the area around them. The trees were closer together, taller, and older than the rest. The more Alex thought about it, the more uncomfortable he felt in what she called the Dark Woods.

"We should do something." Beatrice pulled out her stick —her sword.

"No!" He pulled her back down and dropped his head into his hands, feeling a massive headache coming. "No."

"But it's my duty to protect my people and we're *so* close to them right now!"

"There's no one there," the boy pleaded.

Maybe he could find his way back, he pondered. However, he knew that was just wishful thinking. The boy didn't recognize the "Dark Woods." In fact, Alex was nearly one hundred percent sure that she was just leading him around parts of the forest to show him her pretend kingdom instead of getting him to the entrance, so he was probably further than ever from home.

He was thirsty, sweating, nearing exhaustion, and Alex could see that Rex was feeling the same way.

"Look, Beatrice—"

She cleared her throat annoyingly loud and glared at him.

"No, I'm not calling you that."

Beatrice's eyes raised.

Alex didn't budge.

"Not my problem." Beatrice whistled for Rex and sauntered away from the boy.

Crap. "K-king Beatrice!" The girl smiled and stopped at the sound of her name. "Look, my mom is gonna freak if I don't get home now. You understand. Right?"

She nodded, her spirits dropping for a fraction of a second. "We'll save it for next time, then?"

"Sure," he agreed, not planning on coming back or even taking Rex on a walk ever again.

"All right! Well, we'll have to hurry so they don't spot us! Let's go, Regenald!" Beatrice and Rex took off, leaving Alex far behind and asking himself how those two could possibly have that kind of energy.

Much later, Beatrice came to a halt. "We're here." Sure enough, Alex could see a small trail and even the pavement if he looked hard enough. Overjoyed, he took hold of Rex's leash and raced forward, the promise of air conditioning pushing him ahead.

Having realized he forgot to thank her, the boy turned back, but she was gone. Maybe she was a ghost, or a hallucination from the heat, like a mirage.

"You were gone for a long time!" His mom had been pacing the kitchen for the past hour with worry and had been only seconds away from getting in her car and scanning the neighborhood.

"Yeah, Rex pulled me into the woods."

Marianne teased, "But isn't that against routine?"

"I lost my watch, too." Alex felt the bareness of his wrist and frowned. He loved that watch. It had a beaker and a microscope on it and fit better than any watch he'd ever owned.

"The one from the science center in Hawaii?" his dad, David, asked, entering the kitchen. Alex nodded. "You'd better find it."

"Do I have to?"

His father gave him a look. "You begged your grandmother for that watch. What is she going to think when she finds out you lost it and didn't care to find it?"

The boy groaned. He was hoping that she simply would never find out. "I'll go look for it tomorrow."

Alex hated the idea of possibly seeing the girl again.

CHAPTER TWO

T emerity
(n.) behavior that is recklessly bold

"Just find the watch and leave," Alex repeated to himself, stepping into the woods. He had no intention of staying outside for long that day, nor did he make any plans to bump into the so-called King Beatrice. In fact, the boy would be rather relieved if yesterday was the first and last time he'd ever see her.

His plan was to search for up to forty minutes (ideally finding the watch long before then) and make it back home by three o'clock so he could eat a snack and watch one of his favorite TV shows, just as he did every Monday.

"We wouldn't be here if you hadn't gone crazy," Alex mumbled, bitter as he glanced down at his dog. At least Rex was behaving, though, Alex thought.

Rex was more than happy to be on good behavior. After all, he was getting exactly what he wanted. Rex had never disobeyed his master before, but if that was what it got him, then maybe . . .

With no warning, Rex took off in a dead sprint, nearly throwing Alex down and dragging him along, and then nearly trampling Beatrice as she stepped out from behind a tree.

"Hello, stranger." She grinned and took Rex off the leash. Beatrice hadn't expected for her new friend to come back so soon. The girl ignored the look on Alex's face, the look that said I-really-don't-want-to-be-here-right-now.

"Hi," he grumbled, latching Rex's leash back on, "we're going to go."

"No! Stay and play!" Beatrice undid the leash again.

"I'm only here to find my watch." Alex put the leash back on.

The back and forth confused and angered the lab. Could he explore? Could he not? He was sure he smelled a squirrel close by.

Beatrice felt in her pocket and sighed, "Is it green?"

"Yes!"

"I may have seen it."

"Where? Can you show me?"

The girl didn't want him to take the watch and leave forever. He'd never come back. That might have been the only chance to keep him as her friend. "I don't know."

"Please,"

"W-would you play with me for a bit if I gave it to you?"

It was a trap! How much did he really *need* the watch anyway? Was it so important as to spend another day with her? He would miss his show and he did have work to do. Alex narrowed his eyes on the dirt and clenched his fists. But it was his favorite watch, his dad would be furious, there's no way he'd ever be able to replace it, and he would never hear the end of it from his grandmother. He studied her, the silence carrying on. Her hair was a mess, a few leaves sticking out from the massive curls, and Alex didn't doubt that she put the leaves in her hair herself. He didn't like her ragged appearance, and the hopeful smile on her face almost made his skin crawl. She made him uncomfortable, but she had his watch.

"Fine." He crossed his arms over his chest, wondering what he had just got himself into.

Beatrice was frozen. No one had ever agreed before. Well, more accurately, she had never gone so far as to invite someone to play her game. For a split second, she thought that maybe she misheard him, but he had agreed . . . right?

Out of sheer panic, she dove into it. "All right," the girl stammered, and then cleared her throat. "Mr. Holberry, let's go!"

He marched behind her, making a game of his own out of mimicking her from behind her back.

She led him first to a village she called Lorine Wood. Alex thought it looked plain and frightfully overgrown. There were a couple benches, but bushes and tall grasses nearly covered them completely.

The girl stood proud at the entrance to Lorine Wood, ever so happy to show off their growing town. She loved the tall wooden buildings and the happy citizens who were always running about, dancing, crafting, and living their absolute best lives.

"My good subjects!" Beatrice boomed, her arms stretched wide. Exhilarated, she continued forward, beckoning Alex to follow. Beatrice shook the hands of the lord who was dressed as poorly as the peasants. "This is Lord Turk," she introduced, gently pushing Alex forward to meet the lord.

Alex stood still.

Beatrice rolled her eyes and nudged the boy, whispering, "Go on. Don't be shy."

"Be shy about what?"

"Shaking his hand!"

There was no one in front of the boy.

"Whose hand?"

The girl let out an exhausted groan, "Don't you see him? He's standing right there! You're being very rude. Just shake his hand already, jeez."

Get your watch and leave, Alex told himself, extending his arm and shaking hands with an invisible man in an invisible town.

"My apologies, Lord Turk. This one is new."

The Lord shook his head and smiled, greeting Mr. Holberry.

As they passed the man, she whispered to the boy, "They are quite poor here. That's why a lot of the buildings are run down and they aren't dressed very fancy."

That was why she wanted to take him there first. They were humble in Lorine Wood.

Alex immediately regretted walking out of the house that afternoon. He was expected to interact with Lord Turk, little Anna, and an entire village of people that didn't exist. On top of that, he had to act amazed, or shocked, or whatever Beatrice wanted whenever she showed him the bakery that had burnt down, the swordsmith's workshop, the new tavern . . . all things he couldn't see! If he had to shake hands with one more invisible person, he was going to explode.

"Come on!" the girl cried, noticing him spacing out. He was probably distracted by the town's jester, which was understandable. Beatrice took hold of Alex's hand and started running, whistling for Regenald Rex.

She didn't hold on for long, for which Alex was quite grateful.

"We're going to the river!" Beatrice cheered. Alex found

himself surprisingly giddy to see the river, for he had no idea a river ran through that part of the city. How she described it, the river was huge, the water fast, and one could catch fish as large as Rex in it. The girl continued, "But we have to take the King's Road to be safe, unless you think you're brave enough to cut across."

The King's Road, Alex observed, was the trail they were taking, and perhaps the only one he had seen in the godforsaken place. "The King's Road is fine."

"Maybe later you'll be brave enough to go through the woods!" She smiled back at him, finally slowing to a reasonable walking speed.

"Maybe."

"Ta-da!" Beatrice exclaimed, lunging forward with jazz hands to show off her river.

Alex stopped short, his shoulders slumped, and his excitement vanished. That wasn't a river, Alex frowned. What laid before him could pass for a stream—a brook, maybe—but nothing more. He couldn't believe he had fallen for it. He should have known she was exaggerating.

"There it is!" she exclaimed, looking upon the magnificent sight with pride. When Beatrice stood before the river, she saw its incredible depth, crystal waters slipping into an impossibly deep blue far into the horizon, and its great potential for a boat festival. Silenced by the beauty, she sat down and gazed at the marvel.

"This is your sea? What are you talking about?"

She beamed, "Isn't it magnificent?"

The water probably wouldn't cover his ankles, Alex thought. "Yeah," he said sarcastically, "magnificent."

The girl spoke again. "It's going to be wonderful." Her voice was soft, nearly a whisper.

"What will?" Alex sat beside her, first clearing the space of leaves and sticks.

"The boat festival. Just imagine the river cluttered with boats, big and small, plain and colorful. Everyone in the kingdom will come to watch."

"So, a big event." Alex's interest was feigned, but the girl was too preoccupied on the image of a large ship drifting past them to notice. She waved to the passengers who waved back to their king.

"Yes," she smiled and gazed in quiet contemplation over the river.

The girl played with a dandelion and smiled to herself, drenched in sunlight. Her chest filled with a surge of nostalgia. Her mother would have loved the river. Beatrice looked at the sparkling water as it rolled over the rocks and she imagined her mother dragging her father into the stream to dance and play.

What a nice image, the girl thought glumly. What a lovely dream.

A tear rolled down her cheek, but she wiped it away before the boy could notice.

They sat in comfortable silence as shadows on the ground grew longer, alternating between watching the trees, the impeccably blue sky, and Rex playing in the stream. After a while, Alex even started nodding off. *So much for fifteen minutes*, the boy sighed.

"Have you ever used a sword?" Beatrice asked.

He didn't answer right away. The idea of that girl with a blade terrified him. "I really don't think—"

"Have you?"

Alex sighed. "No,"

"Today you'll learn!"

Goodie, groaned Alex as he followed the girl and Rex to an incredibly neat stack of sticks that she called the armory.

Beatrice could hardly mask her excitement. Not only did she have a best friend, but she had a best friend with a dog. In addition, she had someone to swordfight with. Unable to keep herself from giggling, she looked over their selection a dozen times. She had about seven armories. The girl could never successfully keep track of just one, so she found it safer to have no less than five or six. Beatrice, of course, would take Excalibur's twin, but one of the other large, sharp blades couldn't possibly be safe for someone like Mr. Holberry, she thought.

"Here, Mr. Holberry."

He had half a mind to tell her that he didn't like the name Mr. Holberry, but he bit his tongue. Honestly, he believed that she had forgotten his real name. Alex nodded and accepted a small and unimpressive yet surprisingly sturdy stick. Frowning, he wiped off the leaves and dirt that had stuck to the stick from the last rain. There were no words he could find to express how deeply he despised this idea.

"It really isn't all that hard, but I'll take it slow. Now make sure your grip is tight, but not too tight. If your grip is too tight, then your arm will be way too stiff. Like this," Beatrice demonstrated and helped Alex hold the stick, but all he could think about was the fact that he missed his snack and show on the cosmos to be outside pretending to use swords with some weird girl who probably lived out there in the trees.

"Come on, Mr. Holberry! Hold it right!" Beatrice shouted. "Back straight! Face your feet in the direction you want to go! Head up! How do you expect to fight off bandits if you can't keep your eyes off the ground?"

He didn't want to fight bandits. That was the whole point. However, the girl scared him, so he did as she said.

"That's better!" she cheered, and Rex barked, too. "That's right! Good girl, Regenald! Good girl!"

"He's a boy," Alex muttered under his breath.

"What?"

"Nothing," Alex kicked a stone and drove his hands deep into his pockets. "Look, I really don't want to do this pretend swordplay."

"What? Of course, you do!" She threw a stick for Rex to fetch. "You just have to learn first."

"I think I'm going to go home."

"Your King commands you!" Beatrice moved so quickly that Alex couldn't register what was happening until she already had her stick pointed against his chest. It was a miracle, Alex thought, that she hadn't broken through the skin.

Alex had two thoughts running through his mind: Beatrice was truly insane and if she wanted to, she could stick him through and leave him to die with no one the wiser. Rex obviously wouldn't come to his rescue.

The boy knew better than to say no to someone like that; that's how you got slammed against lockers or all your books thrown on the ground. And out there with no witnesses and a death trap around every corner, who knew what she could to do him.

"I-I'll play for a b-bit longer."

Beatrice's eyes lit up like fireworks and she nearly tackled him in a hug. "Thank you! Thank you!"

"P-please let go."

"Again, Mr. Holberry. Let me see a proper stance this time!"

Alex didn't understand stick fighting, not that he understood real sword fighting either. To make it worse, Beatrice didn't go easy on him, at least not after the first few minutes. There was a look of death in her eyes as they fought, an intensity that, though quite fitting for her, Alex found unnecessary and frightening. The girl would hit harder and harder, and after the second stick snapped, he wondered why they continued.

Beatrice stopped, feeling defeated by his lack of interest. "Come on! This can be fun if you try!" The girl frowned as she looked him up and down. God, he was scrawny. "Pretend a little?"

"That may be more your thing than mine." Beatrice didn't respond, so Alex studied her. He didn't know what he was looking for—a reason to run and go home, maybe, but maybe something else altogether. Whatever it was, he found it after watching her eyes. "I'll give it a shot."

Slowly, Alex grew more confident, or perhaps he simply started to lose sight of his ticks and fears just long enough to have fun. His posture improved, his stance was less awkward, and he attacked with fiery passion.

Beatrice took full advantage, fighting harder than before. Never in a million years did she expect that kind of ferocity, let alone life, from Mr. Holberry.

It didn't last long.

Beatrice leapt from a fallen tree. Her sword struck him, and he fell.

Victorious, the girl roared, holding her sword above her head as Alex cried out in pain.

"Can you stop playing for even a second?" Alex said through his teeth, squeezing his hand as hard as he could to make the pain go away. He was certain his hand was broken.

"Never!" She cackled and hit his back playfully with her sword as she circled him. "I am the king and I have conquered you, Mr. Holberry!"

For a moment, he stared at her in total disbelief as she continued her speech, saying that he'll get better with time and that he did such a good job for his first time, but he was too scared and furious to listen. Her temerity frightened him to his core.

She must be stupid, Alex thought.

"Will you shut up?" Alex cried when his hand began burning instead of healing as he had prayed. That's what he got for not going home when he should have. "You don't care about anyone else around you because you're too busy playing your *stupid* game! You probably broke my finger, but you haven't even noticed because you won't stop talking! You never stop talking!"

"Are you serious?" Her eyes grew fearful as she inched toward him, not knowing what to do next.

"Yes, I'm serious! Why would I joke about that? Stupid." Keeping pressure on the hand, he carefully put Rex on the leash. "Leave me alone."

"But—"

"No. Seriously, don't ever talk to me."

His mother pressed on his finger, wincing when Alex did as if it hurt her as much as it hurt him, which, in her mind, it did.

"It isn't broken." She pursed her lips as she began to wrap the hand with a bandage. "You'll be fine, honey."

His dad tossed him an ice pack. "Put this on it."

"How did this happen?"

"Some girl hit me with a stick when we were playing."

"You let a girl beat you up?" David laughed.

"A girl?" Marianne squealed. "You have a friend? Oh, Alex, I can't believe you have a friend!"

"Beatrice isn't my friend."

"Beatrice!" She sighed, clasping her hands together as she grinned. "Oh, darling, Alex has a friend! Isn't that just so perfect?"

"A friend who beat him up!" David added.

"Be quiet, David! Alex, that's wonderful you made a friend. I was getting so worried."

"Mom, please."

"Maybe we should have her and her family over for dinner sometime! Yes! That's a perfect idea! David, honey, we could grill some burgers and have dinner with her family!" She scurried to a counter, grabbing a scrap piece of paper and pen to scribble down notes. She muttered to herself, "We should have hot dogs, too, in case they don't like hamburgers. Oh! What if they don't eat meat?" Marianne didn't bother to look up at her son, "Sweetie, does your friend eat meat?"

"Look at him, he doesn't want that." Truth was, David wasn't exactly fond of the idea of dinner. He *really* did not want to play nice with a strange couple who were most likely crazier than his own wife, or, worse, dull, or even worse, hippies. He shuddered.

"Thank you," Alex whispered.

"Oh, nonsense! It will be so much fun! Alex, what's her name again? Beth? I'll try to call her mother. Do you think they'll be in the phone book?"

"No. No. No. No. We aren't friends and she is *not* coming over for dinner, Mom!"

"Of course, we are! You're just nervous because this is practically your first—"

"Mom, seriously, no. I'm going to bed. Please, no more talk about this dinner thing."

"Keep icing that finger!" his dad shouted.

As soon as his mother thought Alex was out of ear shot, she said, "We are so having this dinner. What was her name again? Betty? I'll have to find . . ."

Alex groaned and stomped up the stairs. The last two days had to have been the worst days of his life.

CHAPTER THREE

A berrant
        (adj.) deviating from the ordinary, usual, or normal type

ALEX HAD SEEN ENOUGH FACES FOR ONE DAY AND HE HAD only been in the store for six minutes. In his opinion, back-to-school-shopping day was the second worst day of the year (the first day of school being the absolute worst); this was the day when the dread set in. After that moment, there would be no going back. He already knew the summer was over.

Within the six minutes of shopping, Alex had received a total of five smirks from former classmates as if they were already preparing the nicknames and taunts for the year.

Make that six.

"Oh, honey! What backpack do you want?" His mother drooled over the variety.

Alex, on the other hand, stared blankly at the display, not caring for any of them. "My old one is fine."

His father sighed, "You've had that one for a couple years. There are holes in the bottom."

"Look!" Marianne squealed. "This one has those characters you like!"

"It's Space Ghost," Alex and his father said in unison, sharing a quick smirk.

"The black one is fine, Mom."

She looked at her son, contemplating arguing with him over it, but instead put the dreadfully plain backpack in the cart. She remembered getting excited this time of year and wanting so many new and cool things to show off at school, but Alex just wasn't the same. It hurt her sometimes, how different they were.

"Okay, what's next?" She smiled down at her list and headed for the pencils.

Alex was convinced they had been shopping for two hours by the time they made it to the art supplies, which were only halfway down the list, but at least he could enjoy this portion of shopping. For the first time that day, he felt happy, grinning as he grabbed a variety of art sets. Placing a sketchbook into the cart as if it were a newborn baby, he sighed, utterly satisfied, and looked forward.

There she was.

Beatrice.

The boy searched frantically for a place to hide, but his parents were too far away and the aisle was empty. She caught his gaze. Alex froze. He hadn't seen Beatrice in four days, four beautifully quiet days, and he didn't plan on seeing her anytime soon. Apparently, he wasn't as lucky as he liked to believe.

She looked upset, and Alex couldn't help but feel a little scared, fearing the very idea of retaliation from Beatrice.

Why did they have to go shopping, Alex wondered, why there?

"Are you staring at that girl?" His mother had snuck up on him, making Alex jump. "That's your new friend, isn't it?"

Alex could see the wheels turning in his mom's head and he panicked. "No! No way! I-I was just looking at . . . at that binder down the next aisle."

"Oh, I doubt that! Come on, we're going to say hello."

"Honey, let's not—"

But it was too late. She was making a beeline for Beatrice.

"So, what's the deal?" David crossed his arms and glared at the scene of his wife gabbing to the girl and her father.

"There isn't a deal," Alex trailed off.

"Sure, there isn't. What? You like her or something?"

"No! She's the worst."

He chuckled and squeezed Alex's shoulder, pushing him forward, "Yeah, that's what I said about your mother."

"Finally," Marianne sighed in relief. "David, this is Beatrice, Alex's friend, and this is her father."

"Name's John." He shook David's hand, and then studied Alex, frowning.

Alex had never felt so many emotions in such a short time. In the five second pause that John took, Alex went from feeling indifferent to uncomfortable to confused and then he finally felt terrified. He wasn't sure how much Beatrice had told her father, but if she had mentioned how he had yelled at her, then Alex was about to die. Her father looked extremely protective, and he wasn't a small man either.

"So, you're Alex." The boy gulped and nodded, waiting for the man to lift him by the collar and slug him into next week, but the father's expression suddenly and astonishingly turned soft as he grinned and shook Alex's hand. "Nice to meet cha'! Beatrice told me all about you—"

"Dad . . ." Beatrice burned a hole into the floor as she blushed.

"We could say the same about you, little lady! Alex has been cooped up in the house all summer." Alex and his father felt the question before it came out of her mouth, but too late to stop it. "Would you two like to stop by for dinner sometime?"

That was it, thought Alex, his life just ended.

"That'd be great!" John beamed.

The boy could see exactly where Beatrice got her liveliness from.

"You know what, we're about to get our groceries after we leave here. Why don't you come over tonight?"

"Oh, honey—" David tried to protest, a true hero to his son, but she pinched the back of his arm tightly, all the while flashing an innocent smile. "That's a great idea."

The adults went aside to exchange information, leaving Alex and Beatrice to their own devices.

After a long silence, Alex cleared his throat. "I'm sorry." The girl stared at him, making it the first time he had ever seen her with a blank expression. "I-I probably shouldn't have, um," God, he hated this. "Look, you were . . . and I got a little . . . my finger is better." He paraded it in front of her, but her gaze didn't shift. Gritting his teeth, Alex looked away long enough to spit out, "I'm really sorry about what I said."

Alex expected her to grin and giggle. Maybe she would throw her hands in the air, hug him, and tell the boy how happy she was that he came to his senses. He didn't want that, but that's the kind of girl she was. Right?

Beatrice continued staring. Alex couldn't read her, and,

for once, he loathed silence. He felt a shiver crawl up his spine as her eyes gained a deadly presence.

She turned and strode to join her father.

The boy was too confused to move. Why did she have nothing to say? Alex couldn't wrap his head around it. That was why he wasn't friends with girls. They were too difficult to understand.

<hr>

HIS FOUR DAYS OF PARADISE HAD COME TO AN END RATHER quickly. Alex simply wanted a logical answer as to why that girl kept barging into his life, and he wished his mother would have let him take down all the family pictures that hung on the wall. Beatrice most certainly didn't need to see any pictures of Alex, especially the particularly chubby baby picture of him that hung in the hallway on the way to the bathroom.

"We are so excited to have you over!" His mother placed the last bowl of food on the dinner table.

"Of course, thank you for having us."

Beatrice took a deep breath and flashed a refreshing smile, "Yeah, thank you."

Alex piled his plate with food, making sure he made no eye contact with the girl.

"So how did you and Alex meet? I'm afraid Alex doesn't share a lot." Marianne asked as she took a sip of wine.

"At the park down the street."

"You mean that overgrown forest?" His father chuckled, "I never thought Alex would step foot in that place in his life."

"Rex got away, is all. I didn't want to go," he grumbled, wishing that they could eat in silence.

Beatrice grinned, "Yeah, he nearly tackled me!"

"He likes you, that's for sure. He hasn't left your side all evening." And Rex didn't plan to.

Alex glared at his dog and shouted "Traitor!" as loud as he could in his head, hoping that Rex would hear.

Would she tell them her nickname for Rex? Alex wondered. He was on the edge of his seat waiting for Beatrice to blurt out something about her pretend game so that everyone would see how crazy she was, but it was like staring at a candle trying to stoke a flame by prayers alone.

"So how old are you, sweetie?"

"I'm twelve," Beatrice answered through her bite of steak.

"Same age as Alex," David pointed out.

"Do you go to Westmoore, too?" his mother pried, and Alex yearned for the answer to be a firm "no."

"She will be. We just moved here, so it'll be her first year."

Alex nearly choked on his food. *Crap!*

"Well, it's a great school! Most end up going to the best high schools afterwards." Alex suddenly lost his appetite. "So where did you move from?"

"Michigan," Beatrice said. Something seemed off about her, but the boy just couldn't place what it was.

Her father rested his hand on her shoulder and squeezed reassuringly. He knew the look on her face, and it killed him to witness it. "We just needed a fresh start."

Beatrice stood abruptly to leave, her eyes growing watery and red, "Um, where's the bathroom?"

The picture! Alex sank in his seat. *Crap*, she was going to see it and never let him live it down.

"Down the hall, sweetie," Marianne answered.

John whispered to his daughter, "Are you okay?"

The girl smiled big and nodded, but she wasn't and they both knew.

"You chose a great town!"

"We certainly hope so."

"Is it just the two of you?" David asked.

John took a deep breath, "Yes, just me and her now."

Alex felt the air in the room grow unbearably thick and was grateful that, for whatever reason, the subject wasn't pushed.

Conversation continued as his mother brought dessert and Beatrice rejoined the table. Neither of the children bothered to join, or even do as little as listen. They stared at different objects in the room, and while Beatrice tried locking eyes with Alex, he was determined to avoid her.

By the time the parents had ventured into the living room, Alex thought that perhaps he had died and gone to a special kind of hell. Beatrice, however, just hated the silence and the feeling of intrusion. In fact, she started feeling as if the walls of the house closed in on her more and more the longer she sat at the empty table with the boy on the other side obviously ignoring her.

She cleared her throat, "Would you like to go for a walk?"

"Alex used to come down those stairs butt naked—" Alex heard his mother laugh from the other room and he didn't dare wait for her story to finish.

"Yes. Now." He grabbed her hand and wrenched Beatrice from the house.

***

It was quiet outside. Beatrice listened to the rustling leaves, far-off crickets, and the whizzing of cars down busy streets. She found that though the air had a slight chill to it, it felt warm if she didn't think about the cool breeze. The girl had counted the stars, but she could never get past twenty-four before forgetting which she had already counted. There were more stars in this part of the city, Beatrice observed, and she liked that very much.

Alex drove his hands deep into his pockets, frowning. It was cold and Rex kept pulling on the leash.

"I forgive you." Alex didn't have much of a reaction, so Beatrice repeated herself. "I forgive you for the other day."

He stared at her for a minute, wondering why she hadn't just said that earlier; then he nodded.

"So, is this school actually great or is your mom just saying that?"

Alex sighed, not thrilled that she of all people would be adding to his already awful student body. "It's fine."

"Your mom is a really happy person, isn't she?" Alex nodded. Sometimes too happy. "I like her. She's nice." Her words came out as a whisper, "You're lucky to have her."

He shrugged and kept his eyes on Rex.

"Oh, that's my house." Beatrice stopped them and pointed to an average house with . . . was it a garden? It was too dark and they were too far for him to tell.

But, yes, it was a garden. Beatrice and her father had worked quite hard to keep it flourishing in the stead of the elderly woman from whom they bought the home. "It's not that far." She paused, "You can come over whenever you want. I mean, it would be really nice if you'd still like to play before the summer is over."

Alex only nodded, and they continued their walk. He was quiet while Beatrice spoke passionately about this and that. He thought that she was the kind of aberrant person who would pick up an encyclopedia and claim it to be the most thrilling book in the world.

Beatrice was one big puzzle to him. He just couldn't understand what she saw in him. Alex wasn't talkative, he wasn't friendly, he was far from playful, and, for the most part, he resented her, yet she couldn't get enough of the boy.

When Alex retired into the house, their parents still yapping in the living room about God knows what, Beatrice lingered in the yard. The young girl reached into her back pocket and pulled out a folded photograph, something she only carried with her when she was feeling lost. Its edges were worn, some of the color was fading, and there were a few tears from the photograph being folded. She opened it with care, feeling a mixture of relief and despair when her eyes fell upon her mother. The most beautiful woman Beatrice had ever seen. Her mother's smile was bright and infectious. Perhaps that's why the child kept it so close. Beatrice missed her mother. She missed the smell of her clothes, the sound of her laughter as Beatrice made terrible joke after terrible joke, but, most of all, she missed the safety of being wrapped in her mother's arms.

One day, the girl thought.

Somehow, one day.

CHAPTER FOUR

M
isanthrope
(n.) someone who hates people in general; a hater of mankind

Alex kept his head down and slipped through the halls like a ghost. He successfully made it all the way to his locker without being stopped by anyone and was feeling optimistic. Alex glanced at his replacement watch and frowned. Fearing the first-week-of-school traffic, his father had sped him to school early, which meant homeroom didn't start for another twenty minutes, and he had no idea how to occupy his time.

The boy glanced to his left. There was a small dent in the locker next to his. He felt a shiver run up his spine. The dent he saw wasn't the same as what he remembered, oh, so very clearly, but it was more than enough to bring back the horrible day: September 28th of his sixth-grade year.

Pam Truly with her beautiful fiery red hair had strode past Alex and winked at him, maybe because she had wanted to torment him—he knew he could never have her—or maybe to remind him that she, too, had not forgotten what happened. Or maybe it was just because she was vindictive. Whatever the reason, Alex had felt an awful churning in his stomach at the time. The boy had ducked his head and walked faster, just wanting to hide in homeroom.

He didn't like the new school. He especially didn't like that all his ghosts had seemed to follow him there from elementary school.

"Ew! I don't want to date him. He's ugly! Pick someone else." A group of girls had sauntered by, giggling. Alex had turned to face them as he trudged down the hall, wondering if they were talking about him. The girls looked away as soon as they met eyes with Alex, and then they scurried away.

Great, Alex had thought.

Just as he had faced forward again, he saw the back of a boy who towered over him, but Alex had been going too fast to stop. He fell into the stranger who then fell into his friend.

But that had been no stranger. That was Brady Johnson, who already disliked Alex for having asked out Pam Truly, who Brady had desperately wanted to date.

Brady Johnson's lips had crashed into his friend's and they stayed like that for a moment, neither of the boys knowing quite what was going on. But everyone else knew. The whole school knew that Brady had just kissed Aaron.

When Brady Johnson pulled away, shouting and spitting, he probably could have forgotten about the whole incident, convinced his friend it was a mistake, and moved on with his life, but as Brady looked up, he had realized that the whole school had witnessed the kiss, accidental or not. Shaking with rage, he turned to Alex.

"You," the boy had said in a voice that would haunt Alex until the day he died.

Brady Johnson had grabbed Alex's head and slammed it

into the locker, leaving a dent in the metal the size of Alex's head.

Alex shook himself from the memory, still feeling the sting.

God, he hated being at school. It was a year ago, but Brady Johnson never forgot.

Closing his locker, Alex scanned the area. He remembered a nice, secluded corner in the courtyard behind a couple of trees and bushes, so he headed there without delay.

"Oh, my God!" A familiar voice pierced Alex's ears and raised the hairs on the back of his neck.

Before he had a chance to formulate an escape plan, arms were around his neck and an unexpected weight nearly sent him tumbling. That was it, he thought, he was finally being jumped like in the movies.

"I can't believe it! It's such big school, so I didn't think I'd find you so quickly!"

Beatrice. She whipped around from behind the boy and hugged him once more. "But you're here! I'm so lucky!"

Alex wriggled out from her grasped and nodded, not making eye contact for more than a couple seconds at a time.

He could feel everyone's eyes on him.

Beatrice had just finished speed walking through the school and was about to start her second round of searching when she recognized Alex's awkward walk and neat hair. She had been so nervous that the only thing keeping her from breaking down and crying was seeing the boy. She put all her energy into the beaming smile she gave Alex.

"I was on my way to the courtyard," he stammered, walking away from her briskly.

"That sounds cool! I'll join you."

Alex didn't mean it as an invitation, but the look on her

face told him that he wouldn't be able to shake her off so easily.

"I'm so happy that we get to hang out before class! I feel like I haven't seen you in ages."

It was true. After the dinner, Alex had not gone back to the woods and he made sure he never stepped foot on her block. Two weeks had passed. He was hoping that those two weeks would turn into a month, and then that month would turn into a year because, by some miracle, she would have transferred schools at the last second. That dream had been short lived.

"Why is that?" she asked, but Alex only shrugged, too nervous to tell her the truth. "Well, I'm happy that we go to school together now. Who do you have for homeroom? Oh, I hope we have the same teacher! What if we had all the same classes? That would be so crazy! Let me see your schedule! Where is it?"

Alex felt like the entire student body was watching them, and he didn't understand why she was talking so loudly. He wished she would speak at a normal level or, even better, not talk at all. Alex grew tense and gripped the straps of his backpack so intensely that his knuckles turned white.

"What are you doing after school? Maybe we can walk home together. We can go to my house, grab a snack, and then go outside! Oh, but we'd have to get Regenald Rex, too. How could we go to the woods without him?"

Alex listened to snips of conversations as they passed people in the hallway.

"Do you think they're dating? Ew! . . . How gross! . . . Two losers, a perfect match . . . Who is she? . . . Wait isn't that the kid who . . . She's hanging out with him?"

Rage boiled inside of Alex and he felt that if he heard one more word he would explode. He was supposed to be in a silent corner in the courtyard by now, but instead he was dead center in the middle of the exact opposite.

"I think my favorite class is history, but—"

"I-I'm sorry. I should go to class early. I have a . . ." Alex looked around frantically for an excuse, but he came up short, "I have to go."

Beatrice called after him, but he didn't stop. Alex ran to homeroom and took a seat next to the window in the very front, hiding his head in his arms on the desk and praying that the day would be over by the time he raised his head in five . . . four . . . three . . . two . . . one. He peeked at the door, humoring himself, but instead of seeing his classmates leaving to go home, he saw Beatrice. She squealed and ran to him, taking the empty seat beside him. She picked up their conversation from before as if they had never parted.

<hr>

It wasn't necessarily that Alex hated school, but rather that he loathed people. At the ripe age of twelve, the poor thing had a crippling case of misanthropy. He loved going to school. He loved mathematics, experiments, and learning new things. It was people like Brady Johnson who ruined school for him. The worst part for Alex was that nobody saw how awful Brady Johnson really was. No one who mattered, anyway; the teachers thought he was a charming kid. And a charming kid Brady Johnson was—to the right people.

Alex sighed and opened his lunchbox.

When Beatrice stepped out of the lunch line, her fingers gripping the tray, she found that she was shaking from nervousness. Earlier that morning during her pep talk with her father, Beatrice had felt excited, ready to tackle anything, but as soon as she set foot on the linoleum floors and saw the mass of students in the hallway, the girl had felt less sure of herself. She moved out of the way of a group of noisy boys and tried standing a bit taller. Her mother and father had taught her to be brave, but, man, it was a lot harder than it sounded sometimes.

For a moment, Beatrice shut her eyes tight and fought to imagine the cafeteria as the woods, her kingdom. When her eyes opened, her feet were moving and the confident air of King Beatrice commanded her.

A sharp tingle ran the length of Alex's spine at the distant yet crystal clear sound of an awkward laugh which rang a little too loud—Beatrice's laugh. He sunk in his chair and gripped his water bottle with a vengeance. Reluctantly, Alex lifted his gaze from his lunchbox. He watched as Beatrice jumped from table to table, reminding Alex of himself when he tried making friends in elementary, but Beatrice was different; she never once lost her enthusiasm whenever she was rejected, which came as a shock to both Alex and the other students.

Beatrice spotted him.

Alex groaned and braced himself as Beatrice beamed and pranced to the seat across from him.

Had he only looked away a moment sooner, Alex thought, maybe she wouldn't have noticed.

It was too late for that, for the grinning girl had already slid into the seat and erupted into conversation, "I'm so happy I found you!" Beatrice tore into her sloppy pepperoni pizza. "All the other tables were so boring, but, *man*, this food is so much better than what I had at my other school! I mean, it's still school food, but it doesn't taste like a skunk—maybe an old sock, but not a skunk." She laughed and chugged her chocolate milk.

Alex peeked at the rest of the cafeteria, finding, much to his horror, that all eyes were glued to their table. Immediately, he looked down and took a shaky bite of his sandwich.

"I like Mrs. Archer. I think she's so funny!"

Alex rolled his eyes. He knew that Beatrice thought their teacher was hilarious—*everyone* could see that—for she had laughed during the entire class period, much to Mrs. Archer's delight.

"Hurry and finish! I want to go play! What do you want to do during recess?"

"We don't have recess. We're in middle school." Alex mumbled, wishing that they could eat in silence. Why must it be social stigma for people to be silent while they ate? Alex thought. It makes much more sense to simply eat and, Jesus, if you must, talk later.

Beatrice dropped her apple and gasped, "What do you mean we don't have recess?"

He shook his head. Alex thought back to his very first memory, shuffling through all his days trying to figure out exactly what he had done to deserve this kind of torture. Everyone was still gawking at them, whispering their discontent or laughing, especially now that Beatrice was passionately voicing her anger over the "no recess" rule.

"Keep your voice down," Alex uttered so softly it was almost lost under Beatrice's uproar.

"What? I'm not being loud! Besides, I should get to have a little fun if we aren't given recess. Really, what kind of school is this? Do they make the food taste better so we forget that we can't play?" Beatrice's voice had grown louder and louder as her rant carried on, making Alex tremble from anxiety.

"People are w-watching," Alex stuttered.

"Good! Maybe they'll want to join the fun table." Beatrice shook her head. "This is a disgrace! An absolute disgrace!"

The boy stood and slammed his fists on the table, instantly regretting his force, for if the students weren't staring before, they certainly were then.

He looked down to Beatrice, still shaking with rage. She looked horrified. The terror and sadness in her eyes haunted him and churned in his stomach.

"I-I'm sorry."

HE COULDN'T GET OVER HIS OUTBURST AT LUNCH.

Alex had been standing at his front door for forty minutes running his thumb over the length of the dog leash trying to decide whether to stay or go. Rex had been beside him the entire time, running circles around the boy and nosing the door every thirty seconds or so until he finally gave up and sat next to Alex. Poor Rex had been cooped up in the house all day and couldn't think of anything better than a walk with Alex—well, maybe a hamburger, or catching a squirrel, or a car ride . . .

Alex had left Beatrice alone at the table after he apologized to her. She had a look of horror cemented on her face at the time, an image Alex couldn't shake.

Sighing, he put Rex on the leash and marched out the door and to the woods.

It didn't take Alex very long to find Beatrice. She was lying on her stomach out in the open drawing figures in the dirt and spelling out the name Lori. He was surprised when she shot straight up and ran to him with a bright grin.

But it wasn't all joyful. There was pain behind her smile, pain that Alex couldn't see, the same pain she felt during lunch when she had experienced more rejection in thirty minutes than she had in all her twelve years, and the pain she felt as she traced the same name in the dirt repeatedly.

Beatrice wrapped her arms around Regenald Rex and buried her face in his fur that had grown a bit since she had last seen him; not by much, but just enough for the keen Beatrice to notice.

"So," the girl began, pulling away from Rex as she scratched behind his ears, "Mr. Holberry returns." Beatrice removed Rex's leash and strode ahead, feeling better with her wolf companion by her side. Rex, too, was beyond excited to be with his new friend. He loved Alex, that was as true as the sky was blue, but the new girl with curly hair was far more fun.

"It's been quiet today." Beatrice informed, twirling her sword at her side. "I think all the trolls and bandits are hiding."

Alex groaned, not nearly in the mood to be Mr. Holberry today. "That's good." He didn't know what to say to her, but something within Alex told him he couldn't just let it go unsaid because she seemed so different, so stiff and forced. "Are you . . . are you okay?"

She turned and stared at him for a moment. Just when Alex thought she was going to tell him everything, Beatrice grinned. "Of course," she almost sang, swinging her hands by her sides.

He wasn't convinced. "It's just that today, I-I don't want—"

"I'm fine. You worry too much, Mr. Holberry." Beatrice threw a stray stick which Rex stormed after. "My mom used to—"

She stopped.

Alex waited. "Your mom what?"

"Uh," Beatrice shook her head, trying to get her thoughts straight, but her heart was beating so quickly and she felt on the verge of tears. "She just used to say it's not good to, uh, to keep fretting the small stuff. It doesn't matter. It's fine."

Something was most certainly wrong, the boy observed. He almost found it strange how much the incident, if he could go so far as to call it an incident, at school bothered her. "School can suck. Well, not school, but everyone else."

"Why are we talking about school?" She whined. "I have a kingdom to run and you have to worry about keeping up with me."

"You aren't mad?"

Beatrice waved her hand at him and crouched down. "Look," she pointed ahead. Alex saw a dissimulation of birds in a small clearing ahead, but Beatrice saw creatures far more menacing. She saw them standing over a fire, cackling and plotting and oozing, swinging their axes and fighting each other.

Rex was watching, too, from behind the bushes. His tail wagged as his attention jumped from bird to bird. He wanted to attack them or play with them, he hadn't quite decided, but the girl was staying still, so he would, too.

"Goblins," Beatrice murmured, her fingers flexing against her sword. "Look closely. They're there." The girl saw the annoyed look on his face. "It's okay. Just try a little harder. You'll see them."

Alex glared ahead, fighting to see the goblins she saw, but no matter how hard he tried, there were only plain birds.

In an instant, Beatrice leapt from the bushes, Rex beside her and her sword glistening in the sunlight as she raised it high. The girl let out a cry and stormed into the flock.

Alex watched, at first in a mixture of horror and annoyance, and then, as the sun caught her just right, as the birds flew around her, as she spun and laughed and grinned, Alex felt almost mystified by the picturesque moment before him.

Before he knew it, Alex was beside her, chasing after the birds—the goblins—and filling the air with as much laughter as his King Beatrice.

CHAPTER FIVE

V erisimilitude
(n.) the property of seeming true, or resembling reality

"ARE YOU LISTENING? THIS IS IMPORTANT!" BEATRICE PATTED Alex's desk, breaking his concentration.

He hadn't been paying attention to her, for he had been too distracted by her outlandish coat. The outrageousness of it was so extreme that Alex felt too self-conscious beside her, so he made them hide out in homeroom together before school began.

There they sat, Alex facing away from her and Beatrice with her knees to her chest inside the jacket.

"Sorry."

"It's okay! My dad told me I might be able to get recess back."

"How?"

Grinning and practically shaking from the excitement, Beatrice snatched a paper from her backpack and slammed it on the desk.

"What's that?" Curious, Alex leaned in closer and studied the paper that read: We Want Recess.

"A petition!"

"You're really going for this, aren't you?" Alex was surprised that she knew what a petition was in the first place; she didn't seem to excel in academics in the slightest.

"Yup!" Just then a student strode into the classroom, a quiet girl who liked to arrive to class early to secure her seat in the back. "Watch," Beatrice winked and skipped to the girl, paper and pen in hand.

However, Alex had trouble concentrating on Beatrice's encounter when his eyes kept traveling to her coat.

The jacket practically swallowed her whole, but she was comfortable in it. The material itself was navy but so covered in patches that one could hardly recognize the deep blue. The patches were shimmering green, blue, purple, and pink hearts and stars; pastel flowers; and names of bands children their age had never heard of and most likely never would. Alex recognized a few, like Ratt. White fringe framed the bottom of the jacket, reaching the young girl's knees.

All morning Alex couldn't seem to escape Beatrice's name. It was whispered in each class and every student was gossiping about her jacket or the queerness of her personality itself. And though a few girls admitted to admiring her style, Alex heard nothing but harsh jokes about his friend. He kept his head down that morning, especially because if someone mentioned Beatrice, his name usually followed.

At lunch, Alex tried to be brave and not look ashamed when Beatrice sat next to him, but it wasn't easy and he felt a weight lift off his shoulders when she stood to leave after shoveling down her meal.

Beatrice worked with furious zeal as she jumped from

table to table asking for signatures. To Alex's surprise, she got a great many before she was invited to join Pam Truly, Brady Johnson, and their friends. Though Alex was wary of the situation, he still flashed Beatrice a winning grin and gave her thumbs up when she made eye contact with him.

Alex had only looked down for a minute, two minutes at the most, when he felt something off.

He found Pam Truly's table instinctively.

Beatrice looked uncomfortable, and she was. She didn't like that these people were touching her jacket. She hated how claustrophobic she felt as the group at the table swarmed around her and grew louder by the second, asking asinine questions about her beloved coat.

Alex grew tense as he watched Beatrice excuse herself from the table.

He saw it happening before the travesty occurred. He tried to stand, to call out to Beatrice, to warn her, but Alex wasn't quick enough.

Pam's lapdog, Amber, moved her foot just as Beatrice stormed past. One moment Beatrice was walking and the next she was on her face, food and drink from an innocent passer-by's tray splattered everywhere.

It was spaghetti day.

The cafeteria was silent, but it wasn't long before it burst into laughter.

Quaking, Beatrice stood. She was covered from her hair to her knees in red sauce, pasta, and chocolate milk.

"Aww," Pam Truly cooed, "she looks better this way!"

The students laughed louder.

Alex was terrified for those at the table, for he could only imagine the wrath Beatrice could and would surely unleash. But she was silent—silent while the room roared.

As teachers raced to the rescue, Beatrice fled the scene.

Shaking with rage, Alex marched to the cursed table. For the longest time, he said nothing. Alex could only stand there with his fists at his side and face burning red.

"What do you want?" Brady Johnson growled, standing from his chair and making his way to Alex, whom paled in comparison to the tall and strong Brady. "Come to stand up for your girlfriend?" The poor boy shook as he stood in Brady Johnson's shadow. Alex could practically feel his head being slammed into a locker.

Their table erupted into fits of laughter which sickened the boy. The sound sunk into the pit of his stomach and churned until he felt on the verge of vomiting.

"Forget how to talk?" They cackled again.

"S-she . . ." Alex looked away, seeing the rest of the room. Everyone was watching the fiasco and he saw the teachers heading their way. Alex's world started moving in slow motion and he began to sweat so profusely he feared it'd show through his jacket. He had never drawn so much attention, not since the peeing incident years ago. He grew angry and upset that this girl, this Beatrice, could cause such an uproar within him.

"I—" Alex felt dizzy, "I don't even like her." The boy ran, swiping his lunch box off the table, and never looking back.

Much to his mother's pleasure, Alex left for Beatrice's immediately after dinner, however Alex was less enthused; it wasn't going to be a pleasant visit.

Nervous and regretting his impulsive decision, he stood on the stone pathway leading to Beatrice's front door. Alex didn't have the first clue as to what he was going to say to her.

I'm sorry about lunch.

Why are you so annoying?

Is it so hard to just keep your head down?

All sounded like good choices. He glared down the street in the direction from whence he came. Alex didn't *have* to say anything, and he didn't have to be there because, in truth, he owed Beatrice nothing.

Frowning, Alex took a step, driving his hands deeper into his front pockets. No matter how much he despised the girl, after she left school earlier, Alex had been consumed with worry.

Eventually, he worked up the courage to knock on the door.

"Oh, hello, Alex." Her father answered the door.

"H-hi, sir." He seemed so much larger and more daunting than Alex recalled.

"I'm afraid Beatrice isn't feeling too well right now. Maybe—"

"I know. I-I would just like to see her."

John stared down at the scrawny boy. He almost found it comical how terrified the kid looked, which made him wonder why his daughter would befriend such a scraggly kid. But, then again, Beatrice had always been so kind, just like her mother. The father sighed. "Bee!" John called from the doorway. Alex heard a muffled "what?" from deep within the home. "Your friend is here."

Alex waited in awkward silence beside the girl's father until Beatrice trudged into view, a time which seemed to stretch into infinity for both the father and the boy.

Once alone, Alex and Beatrice sat on the front porch patiently watching the sky greet the night. Neither uttered a syllable.

Alex didn't understand this girl. He just couldn't wrap his

head around half the things she said or did or believed. Frankly, he found her absolutely and without a doubt insane, but there he was, sitting next to her. Perhaps it was because she was the only person who saw any good in him, who treated him as an equal . . . though, in all fairness, Beatrice did mostly treat him like her own life-sized doll.

He sighed and glared at his feet, pulling a piece of paper from his pocket and handing it to Beatrice.

Silent, she took the paper and carefully unfolded its damp edges. It was severely stained, crinkled, and slightly torn, but it was her petition. Beatrice laughed lightly under her breath and held onto the paper with all her might, feeling utterly hopeless.

"The jacket was my mother's from when she was little," she sighed. "It's totally ruined."

"I've never met your mom. Where is she? Can she figure out how to fix it?"

Beatrice's hands fell into her lap as she leaned back and stared at the sky, her breathing slow and pained. Her chest tightened and all she wanted was to scream, to break something, anything to not feel so powerless.

The girl sat there for what felt like an eternity.

She didn't want to form the words. It wasn't real if she didn't say it, but that was a stupid thought, which she had been trying to tell herself for months.

"She's dead."

He instantly regretted asking. "I-I'm sorry." Alex couldn't imagine losing his mother. The very idea shook him to his core.

"You know, that's the first time I've said it out loud."

Alex bore a hole into the ground at their feet with his glare. He couldn't think of how to comfort her.

Beatrice felt tears well up in her eyes. She didn't want to

cry, for if she started, she wouldn't stop. Taking a deep breath, the girl tried concentrating on another topic—any other topic—but she couldn't stop thinking of her mother's jacket, and then, by extension, her mother.

Just as Beatrice was about to excuse herself and retire inside, Alex took her hand and ran.

She saw something different in Alex as they fled. He had never seemed particularly strong to Beatrice, and he had not once proved that he had an ounce of bravery in him. But now as Alex held onto Beatrice's hand with all his might, and ran as hard as he could, Beatrice saw such courage from the boy.

They stopped deep in the woods. The two collapsed onto an old marble bench, not bothering to wipe off the fallen branches or pull away the vines.

Alex had taken her to Lorine Wood. He remembered all of Beatrice's special places in the forest, though he'd never admit it to her.

He watched the girl as the sun went down, and she watched her feet. It baffled him how a girl so jubilant and wild was so utterly broken and melancholy beneath that infuriatingly bright smile of hers. And her sorrow was contagious. The longer Alex and Beatrice sat on the overgrown bench, the more he felt her despair seep into him and fester.

A light flickered next to Beatrice, illuminating her countenance for only a moment.

Alex's lips stretched from ear to ear, "Fireflies."

Beatrice lifted her head and glanced around her lazily, not having noticed the light; not having noticed much of anything except the burrowing pain in her chest.

As the moments passed, more fireflies lit up Lorine Wood, and the pair watched in quiet wonder. Yet, for Alex, it wasn't as happy as he had imagined, for the boy had expected Beatrice to be dancing and jumping and giggling with joy.

Beatrice was just as surprised as Alex; fireflies were one of her greatest joys in life, but being in Lorine Wood simply proved too much for her—even the name struck a sour chord.

"Look, Beatrice!" Alex jumped to his feet. "The jester is out!"

It appeared to Alex that Beatrice had slipped away from the world.

She was distracted.

He kept trying.

"Look, he's doing your favorite trick!"

She sighed, "I'm sorry. I really don't want to do this right now."

"Ah, come on! He's doing a handstand and juggling with his feet! You think it's funny, remember?"

Beatrice did remember, but, for the first time, she simply couldn't conjure a vision. She didn't understand why Alex was trying so hard.

Grabbing a stick and pretending to fence, a skill Beatrice taught him, Alex hollered and cheered, desperately attempting to entice the girl into joining.

She knew he hated the game, the whole world she had built. Every time they were together she saw it in his eyes. Yet there he was.

Sighing, Alex dropped his sword and marched to Beatrice, cupping her face in his hands. He had half expected her to shy away—in fact, he hadn't predicted he would ever willingly get so close to her in the first place—but she remained unmoving. "At least enjoy the fireflies. I know you love them."

She gave him a strange look. Beatrice had never told Alex that she loved fireflies. Neither of them had ever brought them up before today, but somehow, he just knew. Her mother would have liked this boy, Beatrice thought.

"Don't let the world hide your light." It was her mother's voice, the most beautiful sound the young girl knew. "You are a beautiful light, my sweet Bee."

Feeling a lightness in her chest, the girl nodded and lay next to him in the grass.

Alex had never taken the time to lie down and watch something like this, no calculating, no studying flight patterns, no hypothesis, just appreciating the show before him, and he was glad he was doing it now. Maybe it was the girl beside him making the pastime so memorable, but he felt better about absolutely everything in the world just then. The boy watched the girl for just a moment. Her world held a sort of verisimilitude. He couldn't quite bask in it like she could, but it was there, somewhere off in the distance and barely visible to him—like a mirage.

"I wish I was a tree." Beatrice whispered.

Alex glared at her, surprised she had spoken at all. "A tree? You wouldn't be good as a tree."

"And why not? They're great and big and beautiful."

"But they're still. They can't jump or run." Alex let out a monstrous groan as he stretched. "Pick something else."

Beatrice laughed lightly, "Fine." She watched the bugs above them. The girl tried counting them, but there were far too many. For a moment, she thought that perhaps this was where all the fireflies came at night. "I wish I was a firefly."

"Better, but did you know that they only live for two months?"

"No," she watched as a firefly flew, one which seemed particularly energetic, and she became filled with sadness.

Life is too short, she thought. Nothing lives long enough.

"Pick again."

"I wish I was a bird." Beatrice beamed, imagining herself flying.

"Pick again," Alex smiled. Beatrice glared at him, almost angry that he was still unsatisfied. "Anything you can think of. What would you want to be?" The boy saw wheels turning in her head and grinned.

"A tiger," she said.

"Louder! I can't hear you."

Beatrice sat up straight. "A tiger!"

"What else?" Alex shouted.

"Hmm," she pondered, "a dolphin!"

"What else?"

"A pirate!" Beatrice leapt to her feet and posed in front of him as if she were already on the ship and threatening the boy with walking the plank.

"Another!"

"A-a mermaid! A-a cloud!"

Alex chuckled, "A cloud?"

"A cloud!" Beatrice pulled the boy to his feet, "So I could make rain! What about you? What would you be?"

Alex pondered for a second. "An aerospace engineer!" He grinned, picturing the small rockets he made now transforming into fantastic machines that would venture into mankind's next frontier.

"Boring!"

"Boring? Do you even know what that means?"

She stuck her tongue out at the boy, "It sounds like a Mr. Holberry thing to say. I wish I was a witch! I would fly high up on my broomstick and cast the most beautiful spells!"

Alex stood back and watched with a small smile as Beatrice danced amongst the fireflies.

She was back.

"A warrior! I want to fight with swords and defeat my enemies!" She grabbed hold of Alex's hands and spun him around in circles. "Or a phoenix!"

"What's a phoenix?" Alex laughed, helping her catch fireflies in their hands.

"A bird of fire! They die in a great big flame and are born again in their own ashes. They're beautiful and great and awesome!"

"That doesn't sound real."

"They are!"

"You've seen one?"

"No! But they exist!"

Alex chuckled, that sounded right up her alley, he thought.

"Name something else you'd be!" she roared.

"An adventurer!" Alex shouted as he leapt for a fat and slow firefly. Even he was surprised by his answer.

Beatrice grinned at him, "Better!" She squealed as she finally caught one of the surprisingly nimble bugs. Beatrice fell to the ground and peeked at the flashing light in her hands.

Alex looked down at the girl and laughed. Her hair was curlier than ever, sticking out every which way, and her eyes were so wide and filled with amazement.

Ever so slowly, Beatrice opened her hands. As she watched the firefly walk on her palms, and then return to the air, she muttered just loud enough for the two to hear, "A king."

CHAPTER SIX

S elcouth
       (adj.) unfamiliar, rare, strange, and yet marvelous

MUCH TO ALEX'S DISMAY, BEATRICE LED THE TRIO INTO THE
woods donned with a cape. She looked ridiculous, but, boy,
did she stride with the most striking pride he'd ever seen.

"Are you sure I can't get you a costume?" The girl had
been asking him for days.

His answer was always the same: "Please don't."

"I can even give you this cape! It's a kingly gift if I do say
so myself. I have another costume my dad and I are working
on. I got the idea from a book I've been reading."

"You read?" He was a little shocked, but he figured that
might be the only explanation for her wild imagination.

"All the time!"

Alex watched Rex as they marched through the woods.
The lab was grinning as always and sometimes running

circles around the two as if to say, "Come on! Let's run! Let's have fun!" But Alex would not be running today, no sir!

Beatrice let out her signature squeal, clapping as she sprinted ahead and disappeared around the bend. When Alex caught up, he found Rex and Beatrice dancing under a tree.

"Mr. Holberry, look! How marvelous!" The girl took hold of a rope swing that hung from the tree.

"How did you even see it from so far away?"

She grinned, "Kingly vision, I guess."

The boy scoffed, "Sure."

Beatrice couldn't have been more jubilant over her discovery of the vintage swing. The wooden seat was old and worn, and with the sun shining just right, Beatrice felt as though she had stumbled upon a storybook. Giddy, she leapt onto the seat, kicking her legs back and forth and humming a sweet song.

Alex didn't like the look of the swing and he swore he heard something snap when she sat down.

The girl swung higher and higher, so high that she thought she could touch the treetops if she only reached for them. At that daunting point, she felt the urge to let go, for maybe something miraculous would happen—maybe the heavens would open and let her in. Wouldn't that be spectacular, she dreamed. She wanted to go to heaven. She wondered what it would be like, but, more importantly, she wondered who she would see there and whose arms she would run into.

Beatrice dismounted from the swing and thrust the rope towards Alex. "Your turn."

The boy had been watching from a safe distance as Beatrice swung. The branch the rope hung from was old, and looked like it'd been struck by lightning in the past. The tree creaked and cried at each swing of her pendulum.

Not safe.

"It doesn't seem sturdy enough," he frowned, tugging lightly on the rope and watching the branch tremble.

"I just did it!"

"That doesn't give me any comfort." He grimaced. "What if it breaks? What if I fall?"

"And what if you don't? What if you soar, grow wings, and fly?"

That seemed highly illogical.

Beatrice stared at him for quite some time before breaking the silence. Softly, she spoke, "I promise that everything is going to be okay."

The boy took a deep breath. "Okay, I'll trust you."

Her face brightened. "You won't regret it!"

His calculations made him quite certain that he would regret it very much.

The tree moaned as he sat on the swing, and Alex winced. What was he getting himself into? He sat still, afraid to move and cause the ancient tree to topple.

Beatrice watched, unnaturally silent.

He gained the courage to propel himself forward and found that if he shut his eyes tight enough, he could block out the sound of the tree's creaking.

When the boy opened his eyes, he gasped. It was beautiful! The swing took him high over a hill and he felt miles off the ground and immersed in a selcouth feeling. Stupendous! He grinned and relaxed, taking in the sunshine.

Crack!

The wooden seat snapped. Alex hit the ground. The boy gasped for air. Something was broken, his back, his butt, something.

"I-I re-regret this. I definitely regret t-this," Alex

murmured, slowly rolling to his side and rubbing his butt, which had landed on a rather large stick.

It was silent until Beatrice erupted into laughter, shaking the trees with her roaring. "A-are you okay?"

"I hate you. I really do," he groaned.

"But you're okay?" she asked through her continued laughter.

He glared at the girl and gritted his teeth, "Yes. No thanks to you."

DAVID NEARLY JUMPED OUT OF THE CHAIR, WOKEN FROM A perfect nap, with the feeling that he had been shot. He felt his chest to be sure, but, upon fully waking up, he realized it was just someone knocking on the front door.

The knocking was so furious and constant that David grabbed a baseball bat just in case.

When he looked through the peephole, the man only saw a little girl. "Jesus," he breathed, setting the bat against the wall. David opened the door, "Hi—"

"Hi! Excuse me!" Beatrice sprinted passed David. "Alex!" She stood still. She heard nothing.

"He's in the garage," David spoke. "It's around the back."

The girl turned back to Alex's father. "Thank you!"

Beatrice burst out of the doors, sprinting through the front yard and down the driveway, making a beeline for the young boy who sat on the floor of the garage, totally unaware of the ambush.

She skidded to a stop and held up the flyer. Beatrice was so out of breath that the boy was afraid she was going to pass out.

"It's tomorrow! We're going!"

Alex put down his tools and glared at the crinkled paper she held. It was a flyer for a parade in town. *Free entry for costume participants* was sprawled across the top.

"Oh, no," he muttered.

"Oh, yes! Most certainly yes!" She spun and squealed. "This will be the most perfect opportunity that we will ever get! There will never be anything better in our entire lives!"

Alex groaned.

"We'll be amazing, Alex! They'll never see costumes better than ours! We'll be the talk of the town!"

He thought of everyone who would see him. Hundreds of people. What if they got in the newspaper . . . he felt dizzy.

"There are so many things we could dress up as." She tapped her chin and paced, "Oh! I know just what I'll wear! But, maybe I should do something different." She turned to him and grinned. "You could—"

"No. Not gonna happen."

She cackled maniacally. "Yes, it will."

There was no winning with her, Alex thought.

Beatrice folded the paper and stuck it in the large front pocket of her overalls. She looked around the garage. It was massive, perhaps even enough for three cars, but it was covered with posters, blueprints, and quotes from people she assumed were scientists, since Alex liked that sort of thing. The orderly shelves held different experiments and all the tools were sorted precisely, not even a piece of paper out of place. His room was a little messy, Beatrice remembered, but apparently, the boy kept the garage immaculate.

"What is this?" she asked.

"I do all of my work in here."

"Your work? You're twelve."

The boy shrugged. "I like it."

She walked to where the boy sat and bent over, inspecting what he was working on. Her eyes went from the plans that sat neatly spaced on the ground to what he was building, back to the plans, and then back to the machine. He was building a rocket, but it wasn't finished yet. What had confused her was everything else that surrounded the rocket and papers. Sure, there were some tools she recognized, but everything else seemed so random. There were scales, metal scraps, water, a boiler, and was that sugar?

Beatrice didn't understand how it all came together.

Alex, on the other hand, certainly knew the correlation and felt comfortable and confident.

"Are you building it yourself?" she asked, peering down.

Alex nodded. "It's the first one they're letting me do on my own. I've built small models in the past, but this one is the real deal."

"How does it work?"

"Basically, the rocket burns a fuel to create exhaust. That exhaust makes the thrust that sends the rocket into the sky. Most rockets reach more than 20 atmospheres which makes them go so high. This one won't have that much. I haven't tested that number on this rocket yet."

"That sounds complicated."

"You get the hang of it. It's kind of like a balloon. All the pressure gets built up inside, and then when you let go of it, all the air escapes from the bottom and sends it flying. Right? That has the pressure of roughly one atmosphere, so imagine that times twenty!"

"Woah,"

"Exactly. There's a ton more that goes into it, but that's pretty much the easiest way to explain it, I guess."

"So, you don't know how high this one will go?"

"As high as I can throw it," Alex sighed, and then with a mischievous smirk, "for now."

"That's not very far."

Alex rolled his eyes at her jab. "My parents won't let me have the fuel I need to send it off."

Beatrice chuckled. "Just put the rocket on top of a Diet Coke bottle and put Mentos in it. That'll be your fuel."

Alex laughed, too, wishing it were that easy. "Hmm, I could use an alternative fuel. Perhaps gelled fuels," he groaned, "but that would take a lot of research." He studied his workspace, frowning as he pondered. "I could use liquid hydrogen, methane, hypergolic fuels, but I'd like to use potassium perchlorate. I just can't go to the store and get those things. I've tried. Or . . . I could get on Dad's computer and buy it . . . hmm, but no that . . ." Alex spoke under his breath as he struggled to come across the most logical answer.

Beatrice laid on her stomach, kicking her legs back and forth with her chin in her hands as she looked about the garage.

"You should dress up as a robot tomorrow."

"I'm not dressing up at all," he muttered.

"Why not?" she moaned. "You could build a cool suit right now!"

"I don't have the time! It's tomorrow! Build a suit before dinner and my show comes on? I'll have zero time."

"What show are you watching?"

"It's on engineering. They build something new each episode."

Beatrice let out an exasperated sigh. "Watch something fun sometime! Would it kill you?"

"It is fun!"

"It's *so* not."

"That's it!" Alex stood up, angry and sick of her knocking on his hobbies. "Let's go."

"Oh! Where to?" She jumped to her feet, giddy about a spontaneous adventure.

"We're going to the store."

<hr>

ONCE BACK HOME, ALEX TOOK ONE OF HIS OLDER ROCKET models from a shelf in the garage and joined Beatrice in the driveway.

"Okay, here's the plan. You'll put the Mentos in the Diet Coke and I'll put the rocket over it, and then we run back. Okay?"

Beatrice erupted into a fit of giggles, "Got it!"

The girl took the top off the two-liter of pop and dramatically dropped the candy in, "Okay, go! Go! Go!"

Nothing happened for a moment, and the two kids felt incredibly discouraged. Beatrice dropped two more Mentos into the bottle and Alex held the rocket as the pop sizzled and foamed.

"Run!" Alex shouted as the Diet Coke exploded, sending the rocket soaring.

The two stood back and watched in wonder as the rocket flew.

It only reached a few feet, but, for just a moment, it blocked the sun and it was the most beautiful thing that Alex had ever seen.

"Now *that* was cool!"

The boy nodded in agreement.

"Is that what it means to be an aerospace engineer?"

Alex smiled. "Yes."

The girl sighed, and then picked up the pack of Mentos. "I better get going," she said as she plopped a candy into her mouth and tossed one to Alex. "I'll be here at ten in the morning. Be ready." And with that, she headed down the driveway. "And you better wear something cool," she shouted from the sidewalk. "Otherwise, I'll be forced to kill you."

***

ALEX GLARED AT THE OLD HALLOWEEN COSTUMES IN HIS closet. He could wear his Han Solo costume, he figured. However, it was from three years ago and probably wouldn't fit. Alex groaned and trudged downstairs. It was 9:50 and Beatrice would be arriving any minute.

The boy didn't fancy the idea of dressing up for the costume parade. He had half a mind to mysteriously disappear on a walk, but she'd find him. She always did.

Beatrice played the front door as if it were a drum, and when the door opened, her face fell at the sight of Alex, plainly dressed in his shorts, laced tennis shoes, and astronaut shirt.

Alex, on the other hand, was shocked. He knew she'd dress up for today, but what stood before him was a level of expertise he hadn't expected. She wore a brightly patterned cloth headdress with beads that hung over her face and a white tunic tucked into dark leather that wrapped around her waist. Her arms were covered in the same fabric as her headdress, she wore pants tucked into her brown combat boots, and gold jewelry decorated her neck and wrists. The most surprising of it all, however, besides the white face paint which dotted her countenance, was the bow and arrows. The arrows were beautiful and the feathers were bright and looked plucked straight from a bird of the jungle.

"You're not dressed cool." Beatrice frowned, disappointed as ever.

"W-what are you wearing?"

"I'm a warrior princess!"

"You certainly are creative."

Beatrice beamed, "It's about time you noticed."

The girl made Alex incredibly nervous on their walk into town. Beatrice kept dragging her feet behind him, getting further and further away. Each time he tried to slow down and match her speed, she would scrunch up her face in a nasty pout and tell Alex to walk his own pace and she'd walk hers.

After a while, the boy almost felt comfort in the fact that the distance between the two made it look like they weren't together in the first place, but that didn't stop the hairs on the back of his neck from standing up. He didn't trust her being behind him.

Zip!

An arrow flew past Alex, the feathers grazing his ear.

His heart stopped.

Was he dead?

The boy froze, breathing heavily and sweating. Beatrice sped past him, muttering, "A wasted arrow." She picked up the arrow and shoved it back into its quiver.

She had tried to kill him, Alex thought. His fingers reached up to his ear, half expecting for the ear to have been cut off from the attack, but there wasn't even a drop of blood. "She tried to kill me," he whispered.

Beatrice sauntered over to Alex, smiling with her hands behind her back. "Why are you just standing there? Let's *go!*" She grabbed on to his hand and drug him behind her.

She's crazy!

When they arrived downtown, Beatrice marched them into the thick of the crowd, something that normally would've suffocated Alex. After the incident on their trek there, however, Alex had never felt safer in a crowd of people.

The girl waved goodbye and ran off, disappearing within seconds to join the parade. Alex tucked himself into the throng of people awaiting the parade, and kept an eye out for police officers in case he had to warn them about the crazy girl with the bow and arrows.

He bought a mango popsicle and stretched out in an empty space in the front row for the very best view. The sun was warm and the breeze was just enough to keep him from overheating. As he was dozing off for a perfect after-noon nap, drums shook the ground and soulful voices unlike anything he'd heard before echoed through the streets.

The boy stood and fixed his gaze on the crowd massing on the road behind the last float.

There were four women dressed as flappers who led the line, dancing and kicking and spinning and grinning. They sparkled in their costumes, and the little girls watching them were going ballistic trying to dance the same way as the women. Behind the flappers was a horde of Storm Troopers, Darth Vaders, and Jedi marching in near-perfect sync. Alex felt just as excited as the little girls as he studied the Star Wars costumes. He should have worn his Han Solo gear, he thought.

Finally, he saw people dressed just as vibrantly as Beat-rice. They were the ones with the drums and tribal songs which seemed to awaken his soul. In the mix of them, the beating heart of the musicians and dancers, was Beatrice.

She had first taken cue from the other men and women who had taken her in as one of their own as soon as they saw her costume, but by the time the girl passed Alex, she danced to her own rhythm. And, God, did it fill Alex with a fire that would never die.

The sun shone on her as if the rays had been birthed simply to illuminate her jubilation, her movements sang of the freedom she felt, and with the confetti that the crowd threw, the scene felt just like a dream to the awestruck boy.

CHAPTER SEVEN

Ostranenie
 (n.) defamiliarization; encouraging people to see common things as strange, wild, or unfamiliar; defamiliarizing what is known in order to know it differently or more deeply

THEY WENT INTO THE WOODS EVERY DAY FOR WEEKS. FOR Alex, it had become more of an adventure than a chore.

He had always just been plain Alex, the awkward kid that didn't like anyone, didn't like the world, but with her in the woods, he was Mr. Holberry. Alex still found the name dissatisfying but it didn't quite seem to matter much anymore. Not when he could be someone entirely different, be someone wild and do incredible things that would otherwise be impossible. And do them with her.

Anywhere else in the world being with Beatrice felt like a horrid thing, but it was different in the woods because life was somehow different. Alex didn't know how to interpret that; he neither hated nor loved the feeling. What he did know, though, was that he loved climbing trees, he loved splashing in the creek with Rex, and he was even beginning to love hearing Beatrice's thunderous laughter. In an instant, it was as if his whole world, all his knowledge and beliefs had been immersed in ostranenie.

"What are you looking at?" Beatrice hid her face, blushing.

"Huh?" Alex shook his head. He had been staring at her. "Your h-hair. It's extra frizzy today."

"It is not!" Beatrice slugged him in the arm and settled a makeshift crown of flowers on her head, "Besides, you cannot speak to your king that way."

Alex rolled his eyes, but bowed anyway.

The girl smirked. "That's better." Beatrice leapt to her feet and placed her hands on her hips, "Come, Mr. Holberry. We have pirates to catch!"

Alex grinned and grabbed his sword, making Rex wild with excitement.

As soon as the two took off running, they were back in their world.

They raced under great trees which towered four hundred feet above them, home to jokester fairies, fantastic birds, and other beasts that preferred to lurk in their shadows.

Beatrice stopped at the sea with her wolf companion Regenald Rex sitting at her side. They watched over the crashing waves which beat furiously against the rocky cliffs.

"There's so many of them."

They looked across the great expanse and saw six pirate ships, but Beatrice was not deterred in the least.

"How do you plan to get to them?" Alex asked.

"Teleportation."

Annoyed, he rolled his eyes. "Teleportation? Really?"

She beamed. "Yup! It's one of my many kingly powers."

Alex frowned. She always gave herself crazy "kingly powers" which Alex quite frankly despised. That's how she won every single game. Should he protest, God forbid, Beatrice would pinch the tender skin on his arm hard as she could —that was what she called her "kingly power of persuasion."

"Fine."

"Close your eyes!" Alex did as he was told as she wrapped her arms around his shoulders and made a strange whirring noise. "We're here."

And, sure enough, when Alex opened his eyes, they were on a pirate ship. The massive ship rocked and water on the deck threatened to knock them off their feet. The smell of blood and steel and rum mixed with the strong scent of the salty sea which waged war beneath them. Three pirates stood before them, all tall, fat, tattooed, and snarling beasts.

"I am King Beatrice, and this is my trusted advisor, Mr. Holberry." Alex waved to the pirates. "This is my sea. I like to think that I'm a fair king. Don't you think, Mr. Holberry?" Beatrice paced aboard the ship, folding her hands behind her back. Alex nodded. "But you've caused me a lot of trouble."

"We aren't going to listen to some girl!" a pirate shouted, drawing his sword and charging the valiant king.

They fought for ages, jumping from ship to ship. However, Alex watched more than he fought, for he was mesmerized by Beatrice's insane energy and how graceful she was despite the water having risen to their calves.

Whenever Beatrice noticed Alex standing still, she would throw a pirate his way or sic Regenald Rex on him, and then, by some miracle, Alex would begin fighting with greater zeal than Beatrice.

By the end, Beatrice sprawled out on the shore, entirely out of breath, and muttered, "We did it. They're gone."

The two remained in silence, watching in the shade as more merchant ships and small sailboats returned to the menace-free harbor.

Just as Alex dozed off, Beatrice grabbed hold of his hand and pulled him to his feet.

"Let's go."

"Where?" Alex brushed the leaves and dirt off his clothes and sleepily followed Beatrice.

"My castle," she smiled, taking him along a familiar path.

The closer they became, the more at ease Beatrice felt. Petals from the blooming trees drifted lazily to the ground and she could hear music playing softly in the distance. There was far more shade near her castle, making the air cooler. Wherever the sun did shine through the patches of leaves, it cast an effervescent aura. Beatrice led Alex and Rex through a bush, over a boulder, and under a collapsed tree, entering the castle.

They strode across a bridge Beatrice had made of stones and laid their swords in one of the armories. The girl dug into her pocket and sprinkled a handful of flower petals on the ground. Alex did the same. Beatrice brought petals every time she came to her castle so she could lay them on the ground. She eagerly awaited the day when the marble floors of her castle would be covered in flowers.

Ladies and gentlemen danced around them. The men wore inventive hats and the women wore beautiful gowns, but a couple of the dancers were not akin to the group, something Beatrice had explained during Alex's first visit. One woman wore a jeweled pantsuit and there was a young man who fancied dresses. Alex never understood that, but Beatrice was always so happy to see them, so he let it be.

"Come sit with me," Beatrice beckoned, leading the boy through the crowd and to her throne.

The throne was huge and elaborate; it'd taken Beatrice several days to build. They looked down upon the castle from their high seat and watched the extravagance.

Slowly, the vision faded for Alex. He couldn't see the cascade of vibrant petals drift from the heavens, nor the elegant dancers. Alex couldn't picture the marble floors or giant windows, but he didn't mind. The boy felt comfortable next to Beatrice on the throne. In fact, it astonished him how relaxing her humming had become. Alex's gaze fell to Rex. The happy lab was rolling on his back in the grass and flower petals, having the time of his life and not thinking once about the terrifying bath which would surely take place later that night.

"This is my favorite spot," Beatrice uttered, running her fingers over a flower petal.

Alex sighed and leaned back. "I think it's mine, too."

She smiled at the boy and realized that she had never been more at peace beside someone as she was right then. It was as if her life was back to normal, her chest didn't ache, and her mind wasn't constantly screaming her mother's name. Beatrice hadn't thought she could have that again.

"Do you see that?" Beatrice leaned far over the front of the throne, her face only inches from the grass.

"See what?"

Beatrice beckoned him to join her close to the ground, but Alex stayed still. Groaning, the girl grabbed his shirt and pulled him to her level. He shouted, gritting his teeth and balling up his fists, but Beatrice paid no mind.

"Do you see it?"

"No," he hissed, "I don't know what we're looking at."

With their faces hovering just above the grass, Beatrice smiled. "The grass. I love the color the grass turns when the sun shines through it."

"I guess."

"Don't you think it's pretty?"

Alex stood and stretched, his stomach growling. "It's all right." He watched her as she gazed at the grass, utterly entranced by the color. "Is green your favorite color?"

Beatrice beamed, "I don't have a favorite color."

Alex ducked under a branch on their trek back. "You don't have a favorite anything, do you? Well, besides your castle."

"Nope. I like everything!"

"Doesn't that get kind of tiring?"

"Only if you have a stick up your butt." Beatrice giggled and stuck her tongue out at him.

I don't have a stick up my butt, Alex thought to himself, grumbling.

There was an annoying buzzing by Alex's ear. He tried swatting the bee away, but Beatrice held his hand back. The bee floated between them, and then landed on a flower atop the girl's crown.

Alex grinned mischievously. "Your dad calls you Bee, doesn't he?"

Beatrice glared at the boy. Sighing, her shoulders slumped and she turned away from him, scaring the bee off. "Don't tell anyone. It's embarrassing."

It was her mother who had thought of the name. The two would garden together, and the young girl's favorite part had been stumbling upon a fat bumblebee lazily jumping from flower to flower and eventually to Beatrice's patient finger. Her mother had been fascinated by her daughter's lack of fear —inspired by it.

"As you wish, Bee." Alex bowed, laughing.

Anger engulfed the girl, a sight which made Alex run. Bee wasted no time chasing him down. At first, Alex thought it was a fun game, which struck him as odd, for he never found running to be the least bit enjoyable. He glanced back, grinning and laughing, but was burned by the fire in the girl's eyes. Scared for his life, Alex sprinted as fast as he could, all the while thinking: *Never call her Bee!*

She tackled Alex to the ground. His head barely missed a jagged rock and his life flashed before his eyes. Alex yelled at Beatrice, but she wasn't listening, not really; she flipped the boy onto his back and pressed her knee into his chest. "What's my name?"

"You almost killed me!" Alex was having flashbacks of when she had hurt his hand and he wished, for once, that Rex would protect him instead of always taking Beatrice's side.

"What's my name?"

"Do you see that rock? It almost—"

"Answer!" She pressed harder.

"Oh, you don't care," Alex groaned and looked away from her. "Beatrice."

She growled, "Wrong."

"King Beatrice," the boy mumbled.

A smile slowly stretched across her lips as she took her knee from his chest and gazed at him tenderly.

Alex felt red-hot and nervous as she reached her hand toward his face, but she only removed a petal that had found its home in his hair. The girl held it on her fingertip for a moment, and then winked at him as she blew it away.

Alex talked the rest of the way to drop off Beatrice, not remembering the last time he had spoken for so long without rest. He told her about new discoveries in science that he found fascinating, his passion on the subject enchanting Beatrice.

The two stopped on the sidewalk in front of her house.

Neither said a word for the longest time until Beatrice's lips stretched into a wide grin.

"I just might marry you, Mr. Holberry."

Spinning on her heels, she raced into the house, leaving Alex on the street with his jaw on the ground.

CHAPTER EIGHT

W eltschmerz
(n.) sorrow that one feels and accepts as one's necessary portion in life; sentimental pessimism

I JUST MIGHT MARRY YOU, MR. HOLBERRY.

Her voice haunted him.

I just might marry you, Mr. Holberry.

If Alex knew one thing, he knew that the last thing he would ever want was to marry Beatrice. It wasn't that he hated the girl, but he'd sooner denounce science than marry someone like her.

Alex studied Beatrice as she arranged the colorful magnets and pictures in her locker. She

hummed a tune and thumbed the beat against the metal whenever she had a free hand. Beatrice hummed a high note —tried to; she sounded like a shrieking bat as far as Alex was concerned.

What it really came down to was this: the boy didn't know what to make of her.

"I'm going home." Alex held tight to his backpack straps and prepared to bid the girl farewell.

"No," Beatrice moaned. "I'm coming with you."

The girl continued situating her decorations.

Alex groaned. "You're just messing with your locker."

Beatrice straightened her mirror and sighed, clasping her hands together and gazing at her work with pride. "It has to be just right." She carefully shut the locker door and linked arms with Alex as they walked out of school. Don't get him wrong, Alex still found physical touch repulsive, but he didn't pull away from Beatrice. In fact, he had stopped wriggling free of the girl's grasp five days ago when he finally decided that linking arms with Beatrice was better than hearing her whine.

"So today we can go to my house and have a snack! My dad just bought new popsicles—"

"I only said I would walk you home," Alex said.

"I know," she pouted, "but the popsicles are so good!"

"You can eat them on your own, you now."

Her shoulders slumped. "But it's so much more fun with you. Some of the popsicle always drips on your chin and I never tell you about it."

Alex frowned, slipping from her grip. The popsicle joke was one of the more infuriating skits of hers.

"I have homework. And you do, too."

Alex had spent every day with her and desperately needed a break, especially with all this marrying business. But, more than that, Alex did have homework. He could practically feel the weight of it in his bag and couldn't wait to get home and start.

"Do it in the morning! That's what I always do."

"That's why you have such bad grades. If you would just—"

Alex fell to the ground, his hands stinging from the rough impact of gravel.

Brady Johnson stood over him, his fists clenched and he was furious.

Alex looked up at his attacker, paralyzed by fear.

"Are you stupid or something?" Brady shouted. Alex stared at the boy, dumbfounded. "If I ask you for an answer in class, you give it to me!" Brady bent down and grabbed hold of Alex's collar, pulling the scrawny boy from the ground. "I looked like an idiot! And—"

Beatrice shook with rage and before she could stop herself, she kicked Brady's shoulder with all her might, throwing him from Alex.

"I wouldn't do that," said King Beatrice, standing tall and unafraid.

Alex, on the other hand, felt silly. He felt useless and weak.

"Oh, you have your girlfriend fighting for you? You're a joke, Alex, you know that? You always have been, but this settles it."

"You're just a bully." Beatrice crossed her arms over her chest and moved to stand inches from Brady, who towered over her. "And you're really starting to annoy me."

"Beatrice, seriously, don't," Alex said through gritted teeth.

The girl shooed him away. "I've got this."

"You don't. Let's just get out of here."

"Alex. Stop." Beatrice glared at him, wishing he'd just shut up and let her help him.

Alex couldn't believe her audacity. She could get seriously hurt and she simply didn't care. And that was exactly the problem Alex had with her—she didn't care about anything. She was reckless and she dragged people into the thick with her.

"Stop acting so tough, like you didn't cry when you got spaghetti on your ugly jacket." Brady pushed Beatrice, sending her stumbling backwards. "You're just a stupid, ugly girl."

Alex froze, for he was familiar with the fatal fire burning in Beatrice's eyes and dancing on her snarling lips.

Beatrice sprang forward. She tackled Brady to the ground. The girl punched him again and again and again.

The two wrestled in the dirt until they finally made it to their feet, fists flying.

It didn't seem like a fight between two twelve-year-olds. There was no slapping, no pushing, but there was blood, and a lot of it.

Alex stood between them, "Stop! Stop it!"

Everything happened so fast. Beatrice and Brady were in such a violent spiral they didn't notice little Alex. The girl swung as hard as she could for Brady as if to end the fight with just one hit, but it wasn't Brady she struck.

Alex swore he heard something in his jaw crack. His hand shot up to his face. A tooth had broken. His jaw had broken. Or maybe his entire face had broken. He wasn't sure, but it was the last straw.

Beatrice fell to her knees, gasping. "Alex! I'm so sorry! I didn't—"

Brady laughed, but it didn't last long. He coughed up blood and gasped as he wiggled a tooth that had been knocked loose.

"I don't think we should be friends anymore."

"But, Alex, it was a mistake! I never—"

"Please just don't talk to me anymore."

The boy walked away from her, the only friend he had had in years, and when she finally chased after him, screaming his name, Alex sprinted home.

EVERYTHING WAS COMING OUT WRONG. ALEX FROWNED AND crinkled up yet another piece of paper. Rex laid beside the boy, looking equally upset, so Alex decided to join the dog in pouting on the floor. The boy picked at the strands of stray fibers in his carpet, wallowing in his weltschmerz and growing more frustrated by the second at the remembrance of the occurrence weeks ago. He wasn't weak, the boy thought, scowling. He didn't need a girlfriend to save him. And for God's sake, Beatrice wasn't his girlfriend! As far as Alex was concerned, she wasn't even his friend. She was too dangerous. He only got hurt around the girl, and that was something the boy couldn't stand for any longer, no matter how much he might miss that silly, stupid girl.

Rex, too, was unhappy. However, Rex wasn't upset for the same reason as Alex—or maybe he was, but Rex couldn't understand his master most of the time. The lab was disheartened because three weeks had passed without going into the woods once. Rex wasn't sure if it was because he was in trouble for barking at that squirrel in the window for two hours or maybe something different.

There was a knock on the door and Alex's father peeked in.

"May I come in?"

"Sure."

Uncomfortable, David shuffled in and sat on his son's bed. He had noticed something had been different about Alex a while ago, but it wasn't exactly that something was different, rather that the boy seemed to have reverted to his isolated self. That's what worried his wife, the son's quiet and introverted behavior, which was the only reason why he was up there speaking to his son instead of finishing some work in the one part of the garage that wasn't covered with Alex's experiments.

"How's school?"

Alex sat up and rested his hand on Rex. "Fine, normal."

"I was never much of a fan of school, either. What about everything else?" He bent down and unraveled a crinkled paper that was left on the ground. David looked at his son's design. It seemed he was sketching out the mechanics for a space station of sorts. "How are the designs coming along?"

"Slow," Alex grumbled. "I'm not there yet."

"You will be. One day."

"Soon, hopefully."

The two were quiet, awkwardly sitting and not knowing what to say.

"Are you happy?" David hated the words as soon as they were uttered. He had never been much of a talker, and he wanted to approach his son in a different way than his wife had been, but he wasn't making much progress.

"What?"

"You've been quieter lately. Your mother noticed it and she's worried. You just haven't been acting like yourself."

"I've been acting exactly like myself," Alex combatted, feeling slightly offended.

David nodded and stood to leave. "You spend so much time inside. You have the rest of your life for that. Go out and be young while you still can."

PART TWO

5 Years Later

CHAPTER ONE

N epenthe
(n.) anything bringing a pleasurable sensation
of forgetfulness, especially of sorrow or trouble

ALEX SHUT THE DOOR TO HIS CLASSROOM BEHIND HIM AND
breathed a sigh of relief at the barren hallway. Hands deep in
his pockets, Alex trudged to the bathroom, practically dragging his feet.

The bathroom was empty, too—perhaps the only sign of
good luck Alex had seen all week . . . or, rather, would've
been, if the boy believed in luck.

Alex didn't understand all the rumors about the men's
restroom smelling awful, he thought as he stood in front of
the mirror. The bathroom smelled good. Clean. The girls',
however, probably did smell terrible, considering their
monthly whatever-it-is that they dealt with (Alex knew
perfectly well what it was, but he hated thinking about it).
Though now that he was on the subject, he realized there was

one men's bathroom on campus he always steered clear of;
one stall forever remained indisputably pungent.

The boy dampened a paper towel and scrubbed the red
spot on his shoulder. Mumbling a curse under his breath,
Alex threw the paper towel in the sink. The red stain was
spreading. It astounded Alex that despite being in their senior
year, Brady Johnson still found pleasure in throwing various
objects at him. The object had been a—well, Alex wasn't
quite sure what it was this time, but what he did know was
that it was red and that it had stained his new shirt.

Sighing, he threw the paper towel away and marched out
of the bathroom. He was going to have to change classes
—again.

When the period ended and the bell rang, Alex was running
terribly behind. Every other day he was out of the door and sitting
in his other classroom before the hall rush ever had a chance to
begin. Sure, he was always out of breath by the time he reached
the next room, but he figured it was well worth it. However, that
day his teacher had continued lecturing through the bell.

Alex felt sick at the sight of all the students in the hall. It
was a horde of gossiping bodies moving at the slowest pace
possible and filling the air with a horrid mixture of odors, but
Alex much preferred to call it hell.

Holding on to the straps of his backpack for dear life,
Alex braved the storm.

He saw her.

She was a wave crashing upon a shore, a terrifyingly
gorgeous display of beauty, tranquility, serendipity, and chaos
all at once.

She was nepenthe.

She struck a chord within him, a chord that sounded a
euphoric melody and a hideous ringing that shook him to his

core. The boy didn't know whether to run from her or to her, but when she turned, her bright eyes grazing over him for just a second, nothing else seemed to matter. She smiled and Alex couldn't think of a more spectacular view.

The girl reminded him of a poem.

"Move!"

Alex was thrown into the thick of the crowd.

"Don't just stand there!"

She was gone.

IT WAS AS THOUGH HE HAD SEEN A GHOST.

Alex tapped his fingers on the dining room table later that evening. The table was cluttered with college applications, but he had stopped paying attention to them long ago. It had only been a second that he had seen her, but Alex couldn't stop thinking about it. There was something familiar about the girl, like he knew her, but that couldn't be possible. She was gone. She had been gone for years, but that face . . . he knew those eyes.

"What sounds good for dinner, sweetie?" his mother cooed to his father, striding into the kitchen, David just steps behind her.

"I don't think I'm hungry."

"Of course, you are. You're always hungry," David chided with a chuckle, peering into the refrigerator and frowning.

"Nothing sounds good." Marianne sighed, crossing her arms over her chest.

"Chinese?" David suggested.

Rex sat beside Alex, wagging his tail.

The boy stared at the dog, the memory of the girl growing more and more clear the longer he watched.

"You can't say no to every restaurant I pick," David groaned.

"It's not my fault you're only naming bad places."

"You're so picky! Why don't we go to that place on 6th and Ebon? You love their food."

"Perfect." She smiled and took her husband's hand. "That wasn't so hard, was it?"

"Oh, just go put on your shoes."

"I-I'm going for a walk," Alex murmured, grabbing Rex's leash.

"Go when we get back. We're leaving right now as long as your mother doesn't get distracted in the bathroom."

"I'll make a sandwich later or something. Have a good meal."

"You're sure?" His mom peeked into the room as she put on her earrings, "And David, I heard you."

THE BOY CAME TO A STOP AT THE EDGE OF THE WOODS. REX was nearly jumping for joy, but Alex felt queasy. It had been five years since he came into the forest, and it almost felt forbidden to enter without Beatrice waiting somewhere deep within.

Beatrice.

Alex hadn't thought of her in ages. Her name felt foreign on his lips.

With trepidation, he gripped the leash and marched onto the path.

Alex had forgotten how much he missed the forest until he started recognizing parts of Beatrice's world. Each path was overgrown and trees that used to stand perfectly erect and strong had fallen over from storms. The woods seemed sadly abandoned as if Alex and Beatrice were the only things that had kept it alive all those years ago.

Seeing how the branches twisted and turned, how the flowers stretched through the overgrown grass, and how the sunlight seemed to shimmer as it broke through the leaves, Alex remembered the poem the girl from the hallway resonated.

It was in a flash
that the two souls met.
And in that flash,
so inconceivably insignificant,
yet impeccably important,
the heavens came down to kiss the Earth
and the universe exploded in jubilation.
How peculiar that the love
of just two beings
can shake the entire consciousness of mankind
and it all happen in a flash.

Rex's tail wagged ferociously. He caught onto a scent he hadn't smelled in years, an aroma he loved. The dog pulled hard on the leash, dragging the poor boy behind him and giving Alex an overwhelming sense of déjà vu.

The rock perched before the boy and his dog was massive and Alex recognized it immediately. Slowly and hesitantly, air caught in his lungs as his gaze traveled from ground to sky.

There, surrounded by flowers atop the boulder, sat a girl. She had long curls that billowed gently alongside the soft wind and she hummed so gingerly that the tune was almost lost in the air.

Frantic, Rex barked and broke from Alex's grip, racing to the girl. The lab leapt to the top of the rock, as uncoordinated as he'd ever seen the dog since his puppy stages. Petals flew in every direction and the girl laughed as Rex licked her and barked, throwing himself into her and nearly knocking her to the ground.

Everything settled as Rex's barking died down.

Her voice was delicate and drifted until it reached Alex's ears. "It's been years."

The girl stood, flowers pouring off her as she gained her height.

The shock of it all was almost enough to knock Alex off his feet. It felt like a dream to the boy as the sight in front of him molded into the image of a small girl standing proudly with hands on her hips, chin up, frizzy hair, and a smirk. But when the memory faded, blown away by a gust of wind, Alex didn't see a small girl anymore; rather, he saw a woman. She was tall, grown into her awkward body, and her curly hair had been tamed and now framed her face. Alex didn't feel frightened looking up at her as he had all those years ago; she appeared far sweeter than before—perhaps because she wasn't flashing a malicious smirk or pressing a sharp stick into his back.

"This is the same place where I first met you. Isn't it?"

The boy nodded, scrambling for words.

Beatrice, he thought. *It's really her.*

She smiled fondly and reached down to scratch Rex behind the ear. Beatrice averted her gaze from Alex and focused on Rex. She didn't know how to feel at that moment. She wanted to punch the boy, for she had never forgotten the last day they spoke or how it felt to be ignored by the one friend who ever showed her affection. And yet she desperately wanted to run to him, to hold him, and to cry.

Breathing deeply, the girl studied Rex, feeling an overwhelming wave of sorrow as she ran her fingers through Rex's gray fur. *He's getting old*, Beatrice thought.

"I saw you today," Alex muttered, finding it strange and almost a betrayal to his old self that Beatrice had been the girl in the horde of students. "You go to my school."

"Do I really?" She laughed lightly, climbing off the rock and resting against the trunk of the tree next to Alex. "Funny how things work out, huh?"

He nodded.

They remained in silence, listening to the rustling of leaves and the heavy panting of Rex. Beatrice couldn't shake the uncomfortable feeling she had being close to the boy. She vaguely remembered wanting nothing more than to be by his side, but that was a long time ago, and she had changed since then.

"What happened to you?" Alex asked, peering at her.

"I left. My dad and I moved to a different city before Christmas because I couldn't handle the kids anymore. It just got too much for me after my fight with Brady. But you were there. You remember."

"I was stupid. I should have done something." Alex balled his hands into fists and grimaced at the memories.

Beatrice took a deep breath. "You were a kid. We all were." She smiled at him sweetly and in that one gesture, Alex felt forgiven and finally at peace.

"What have you been up to?"

"Well, I'm in the theater now. It's pretty much all I do."

"Theater," Alex chuckled, "that makes a lot of sense. I bet you're really good."

"I don't know about really good, but I'm trying." Beatrice thumbed through a small stack of petals she took from the rock, sifting through the memories she still had from five years ago. "And . . . y-you're still building models?"

"They're more practical now. I've made a few robots and hopefully in the future I'll help construct spacecraft."

"You're just as I remember you. You just look older." She smiled as she touched his cheek, running her fingers over the beginnings of his beard. Her touch sent a chill up his spine. "Do you remember when we used to come here all the time?"

Alex nodded. "I miss it sometimes."

She held her smile and looked down at Rex. Laughing nervously, she said, "I miss it a lot. Almost every day. God, what was your name?"

Alex groaned and rolled his eyes. "Mr. Holberry."

"Right! *Wow*, I really had a strange imagination."

"And you were King Beatrice." Strangely, the boy felt better beside her, sitting next to his childhood friend and reminiscing in their nostalgia. He had missed her terribly, even though he felt odd admitting it.

"You have an amazing memory. You know that? I'd kill for that when it comes to memorizing plays."

"Thanks."

Beatrice fixed her gaze on Rex, pensive and her brow furrowing, but then her frown turned into a bright smile, the smile Alex always remembered her having. "Regenald Rex, my trusty wolf."

"You wanted him to be a girl," Alex grumbled, rubbing Rex's stomach.

"Regenald's sex didn't really matter to me. I just thought it was funny seeing you get all worked up about it."

"You only liked to see me angry."

Beatrice laughed, "One of your veins used to pop out. Seeing it was one of the simple joys in life."

The girl watched the sun slowly set through the breaks in the trees and Alex watched her.

They were a strange pair, the two of them; they knew each other so well, yet not at all.

"Well, I guess I'll see you at school." Beatrice stood to leave.

Alex felt frantic. "Wait! Did you move back to the same house?"

She nodded. "The one with the stone steps."

They boy watched Beatrice leave, and Rex pulled on the leash, wanting to follow his old friend home.

Alex felt utterly amazed, dumbfounded, flabbergasted, the whole armada.

It was her.

And the years had changed them.

CHAPTER TWO

L achrymose
        (adj.) suggesting of or tending to cause tears;
mournful

ALEX WAS UNPLEASANTLY HOT. HIS SKIN TINGLED FROM THE heat, but he much preferred hiding out in the less-crowded courtyard than ducking for cover in the cafeteria or in the commons.

The real reason why Alex braved the heat was Beatrice. She, too, was out in the blistering weather, though Alex doubted she was bothered by it. He watched her from the seclusion of his bench. Beatrice was surrounded by people and laughing. Her laugh was still the same, still obnoxiously loud, but it felt genuine to Alex. The girl seemed incredibly happy, which filled Alex with relief. He was glad to see her with friends who accepted her.

Beatrice's group acted eccentric, making faces, laughing far too loudly, and wrestling with each other. She fit right in.

Alex couldn't help but notice how much she had changed.

She presented herself with ease, comfortable in her own skin, but perhaps that wasn't it at all, Alex thought, for she had always been comfortable in her skin. She just hadn't felt safe before.

It saddened him that her hair was no longer a frizzy mess. He laughed to himself—he didn't know how else to make fun of her now.

She had grown into those big eyes of hers, Alex observed, and she looked beautiful, as peculiar as it was to admit. He felt nervous at the realization and shifted uncomfortably on the bench.

Alex couldn't say the same for himself. He felt as though he hadn't changed. He was still the scraggly boy who sat alone and wanted nothing more than to avoid the world, but he didn't mind that so much. One thing was certain: he missed that strange girl.

Beatrice's gaze fell on Alex, and she withdrew from the conversation. For a moment, it was as if she was back in the middle school cafeteria seeing Alex sitting awkwardly and isolated at his table.

"I'll see you guys later," Beatrice said, taking her bag and striding towards the boy who sat on the other end of the courtyard.

"Where are you going?"

"See you at rehearsal?"

"Yes," she laughed, "I'll see you guys at rehearsal!"

Beatrice plopped down next to Alex, chuckling at the alarm on his face.

He hadn't the slightest clue as to why he felt so frightened of her—perhaps it was force of habit.

"What are your plans tomorrow?"

"It'll be Saturday," he paused, "so nothing."

Beatrice grinned, "Ah! You have a sense of humor now! Well, I was thinking that we could get together."

His palms began to sweat and Alex's heart pounded so hard he thought he was going to pass out. "W-would you like to get dinner?" He didn't know if that was the right thing to say and he felt drowned by his anxiety.

"That sounds nice," she smiled, "but I was kind of thinking that the woods were more our style. I'll see you there at four!"

A DEADLY CONCOCTION OF DREAD AND EXCITEMENT CHURNED in Beatrice's stomach the deeper in the woods they went. She looked to the boy beside her who somehow managed to stumble every few paces and was sweating up a storm. Some things never change, she thought.

"I remember this place." To Alex, her smile seemed strangely sorrowful.

Beatrice ran her fingers over the low-hanging tree branches she passed.

"Where are we?" Alex peered.

The trees were tall and thin and sunlight drenched the three travelers, casting a mystical aura.

Beatrice whispered, only remembering the words as they left her lips, "Lorial Pass."

"I don't think I remember this place."

"You will," she smirked and followed closely behind Rex who seemed to know exactly where he was going.

The towering trees and seclusion from the modern world reminded Beatrice of stories.

"I've been doing a lot of reading since I left."

"Of what?"

"Mythology mostly."

Alex smiled. A part of him hoped that perhaps she would say something along the lines of astronautics, but mythology seemed so much truer to her person.

"Have you heard of Valkyries?" Alex shook his head. "Really? I'm surprised, Mr. Know-it-all," she chuckled. "They're from Norse mythology, mostly. Valkyries are these great winged women who are both beautiful and terrifying. During battles, they fly down from the sky and carry off the dead. When rays of sun pierced the clouds, they believed the Valkyries had arrived. There's so much more, like how they influenced battle, blah blah blah, but I always thought it would be fascinating to look up into a stormy sky and just as the light breaks through the clouds, see a Valkyrie." Her shoulders slumped in longing.

"But wouldn't that mean you'd be dead?"

She was quiet, lachrymose as she longed for the sky and its bevy of terrible angels. "I don't know, but maybe that wouldn't be such a bad way to go." She sighed. "All I know is my adventures would have been much more brilliant had I only known what those things were."

Beatrice spoke to the boy of all the great stories and creatures she had studied, and her eyes sparkled with liveliness as her passion bloomed.

At the end of Lorial Pass was an overlook of the city, a view Alex couldn't fathom how he had forgotten. For quite some time, Alex gazed over his city, relishing the sight of the far-off buildings, parks, and homes that were below. His eyes landed on Beatrice. She seemed to be experiencing a scramble of emotions that he didn't understand. It was like some unseen atmospheric pressure was crushing her and making it hard to breathe, or as if she was fluctuating between the need to laugh or cry. Rex came to the rescue, nudging her hand with his nose and grinning up at her.

The girl knelt beside the lab, her Regenald Rex, and felt immediately relaxed. "Thank you," she whispered into his fur.

Her voice broke the resting silence. "I miss being able to see the things I used to imagine."

"Could you ever see them?"

Her lips curled into a smirk, "Occasionally."

"I believe you could again."

"Do you see them? The towers? The sea? The fairies of Lorial Pass?"

He stammered, "Isn't it a little silly to still search for those things?"

"I don't know. Maybe not."

Beatrice glided to a tree a few paces away. The girl ran her fingers over the bark as carefully as if it were a piece of glass. Air caught in her lungs as her fingertips followed the indentions of the letter *L* that had been carved into the tree. She remembered that letter, for she had carved it herself with a knife stolen from her father. And though it had pained the young girl to cut into the tree, she had needed the name that the letter represented to be embedded into the essence of the forest as much as she needed to breathe.

Beatrice smiled at the thought of her younger self. She had been so desperate then. She was desperate still.

"Perhaps we could adventure again." The girl turned from the tree to face her friend, "For old time's sake."

Alex saw the hunger in her eyes, "I-I wouldn't know how to begin."

"It seems a bit awkward now. Doesn't it?"

Alex nodded. *Awkward to say the least.*

Beatrice slumped against a rock, her face in her hands as she pouted and pondered.

Alex let out long, slow breaths and as he allowed his mind to wander, he remembered that a new episode of an intriguing TV series came on that night. He glanced down at his watch. The episode started in exactly four minutes.

"We aren't old yet. It can't be that hard!" Beatrice exclaimed as she jumped to her feet, held fast to Alex's hand, and took off in a dead sprint—a pace at which Rex struggled to maintain.

Beatrice stopped so suddenly that Alex nearly fell and crashed into a tree, but she paid the mishap no mind, which was no surprise to him. "The sea, Mr. Holberry!" Beatrice kicked off her shoes, a mighty stick in hand, and leapt into the sea, pushing past the giant, salty waves.

Alex chuckled at the sight, happily staying on dry land. The creek had risen since he had last seen it. The water now rose to Beatrice's knees.

"Do you still remember how to fight?"

Alex sighed. "Not this again."

A weight sunk in the girl's chest as she stared at the reluctant boy whose hands were deep in his pockets and eyes cast away. She felt nervous. Perhaps she shouldn't push so hard to revive their past. Beatrice felt stupid as she watched him, her pants soaking wet, but something told her not to give in just yet.

"Don't make me feel silly, Mr. Holberry. It isn't gentlemanly of you."

Alex frowned, slid his shoes off, carefully tucking his socks inside, and searched for a stick.

He had most certainly forgotten how to fight. However, Alex was regrettably unaware of that fact as he marched into the water with a cocky grin. With the girl's first strike, Alex was off his feet and fully submerged in the water.

"I suppose it isn't entirely fair. I've taken lessons." She winked and offered him her hand, but he refused her help.

The girl appeared harmless and perfectly sweet, but she was insane, a fact that Alex had forgotten. He remembered now, though. He remembered every threat, every cut, and every bruise she had given him in their short time together those five years ago.

Alex eyed Beatrice as he stood, struggling between going with his gut and forfeiting or siding with his pride and continuing. He found his answer in the hope that lit her eyes.

The two were chaos as they roared and laughed and waged war in the sea. The harder they fought, consumed by adrenaline and dripping with sweat, the less of the world around them could they see. For the first time since they met, they were perfectly synced and saw the exact same reality—terrifying waves, distant mountains, and a sun that devoured the sky.

Alex fell, yet again defeated by the storm of a girl. She smacked his arm gently with her sword and smirked. As Beatrice reached to help the boy, she froze, her eyes glued to a point beyond him.

"A great water spirit," she uttered.

The words left her lips and her concentration faltered instantaneously. The sea vanished and the sun shrunk behind the trees. The abrupt absence of their world was enough to knock the air out of her lungs.

Beatrice wanted to see the great spirit. The water before her spat and bubbled, but it never rose enough to embody the terrifying spirit she had conjured.

Alex looked to the girl. She stood completely still, kneeling and glaring ahead. He waited for her to describe what she saw. A water spirit, she had claimed, but the boy didn't know where to start with drawing up a creature such as that; he had always relied on her detailed descriptions to breathe her imagination to life. Beatrice's lips quivered as if she wanted to speak but couldn't find the words.

"I see it," he lied.

Beatrice's voice barely reached him, "W-what does it look like?"

He gulped. Alex only saw the creek and trees and Rex lying down by a pile of sticks and pine cones. Shutting his eyes tight, Alex envisioned what he believed twelve-year old Beatrice would see. "The spirit is rising up from the water. The waves stretch to mold into a giant and its eyes are shining, like it can see right through you. It's loud, almost as if a storm is forming." Alex peeked at the girl. Her eyes were closed and lips pursed as she used all her energy to envision his words. "It's coming close. The spirit is bowing to you. Bow back."

The girl did as she was told.

He whispered, "You can stand up now. It went back into the water."

She was still, her eyes closed. "Thank you," Beatrice muttered under her breath, too quietly for Alex to hear. The girl strode from the creek and slid her shoes back on her feet. "Let's go. I'm hungry."

"Have you not eaten?"

"Nope."

"Have you eaten at all today? Lunch?"

"Nope, we had a weekend rehearsal, so I drove over as soon as we finished."

"You're as irresponsible as ever."

Beatrice gripped the wheel and sighed once she saw Alex and Rex disappear into the house. She couldn't stop thinking about the water spirit. Perhaps she had lost who she used to be, the wide-eyed girl who refused to let the world tear her down, but what pained Beatrice was that she didn't know if she missed that part of her.

But if she let go of that, grew up, so to speak, and left it all behind, would she in extension be letting go of what reminded her of her mother? That was what she feared losing the most.

She punched the wheel and screamed through her gritted teeth, her head falling back against the head rest.

Would there ever be a day she wouldn't think about her mother? Would there be a day she wouldn't feel pain?

She took a deep breath and exhaled painfully. Her chest shook and the dam in the girl's eyes threatened to break.

Would it ever stop? Would it ever get easier?

Shifting into gear, Beatrice drove home, a sick feeling churning in her stomach. She had changed over the years, far more than Alex could have imagined. That little girl was gone forever.

CHAPTER THREE

D uende

(n.) charm; magnetism, the ability to attract others through personal magnetism and charm

Alex didn't have time to blink before he was ripped away from the courtyard and dragged to the parking lot by a very determined Beatrice.

"Hey, guys," Beatrice said as she climbed into the vehicle. "I brought a plus one. This is Alex."

"Welcome! I'm Troy, this is Marie, and transportation today is provided by Road Warrior." The toothy-grinned boy behind the wheel turned and shook Alex's hand.

"God, do you *have* to call your Jeep that?" The girl in the passenger seat rolled her eyes, and then smiled to Alex.

"I like it," Beatrice winked.

"And that is why we're friends." Troy and Beatrice chuckled.

Usually, Alex sat in the courtyard—no, not usually,

always—on the same lone bench and ate his lunch before heading off into the computer lab, but as he looked to Beatrice who had her hand out to help him into the Jeep, he realized he didn't have much of a choice today.

To Alex's discomfort, the Jeep was small and had no covering, so Alex sat upright in his seat in the back—which was technically the vehicle's trunk—across from Beatrice. When Troy came to one particularly harsh stop, Alex was certain he'd meet Death on the concrete beneath them.

Beatrice, on the other hand, found the ride thrilling as always and thought the horrified expression on Alex's face was entertaining. She was glad she had decided to drag the boy along with her. Watching him sit by himself nearly broke her heart. He was a nice boy and she simply wished that others could see that, too. But, more than that, she wished that Alex would give others the chance to impress him.

"How does Mexican sound?" Troy asked as he turned left.

"No, what about Italian?"

"I'm sorry," Troy shouted far too loudly, "the wind is *so* strong. I can't hear you! I think you said Mexican!"

"No Mexican!" Marie yelled.

Beatrice giggled as Troy turned into a parking lot and grinned, "I'm so glad y'all said you wanted Mexican."

"Whatever. Tomorrow I'm driving and where we eat will be put to a fair vote."

"My car, my pick."

The two bickered all the way into the restaurant which entertained Beatrice to no end.

To Alex, however, the constant hammering of Troy and Marie's voices only served to annoy Alex.

"Lighten up, Alex!" Beatrice linked arms with him and whispered, "Enjoy the company."

The restaurant was bustling. Nearly every seat was filled

and with the sound of music and every teenager in the city having lunch there, it was impossible to have a quality conversation. He studied the decorative ceramics on the wall, and then fixed his gaze on Beatrice who sat across from him in the booth. She scarfed down chips and salsa like an animal.

Alex didn't say much during lunch, a few sentences at most. He mainly watched and listened.

There was a moment when Marie, who was for some reason sitting next to Alex and bumping into him every fifteen seconds, claimed that Beatrice was perhaps one of the sanest people she knew. At that moment, with a wink from Beatrice, Alex knew that he had seen a side of the girl that no one else had. What would they think, he wondered, if they knew she called herself King?

Abruptly, Beatrice sank into her seat and blushed, head cast down but eyes glued to a point somewhere beyond Alex.

Marie kicked Beatrice's foot under the table and squealed, "Oh! Who do you see?" The girl scanned the restaurant. "Is it him?"

Troy seemed to perk up as he joined in the manhunt. "Where?"

Beatrice shook her head and slid deeper into the seat.

Alex had never considered the girl having a crush; romance had never been part of her adventures.

"Tell us!" Marie begged, bumping Alex yet again as she pleaded. Alex scooted to the edge of the seat. One of his legs nearly hung off the side.

Beatrice took a deep breath and a small smile formed on her lips as she pointed ahead of her, so nervous that she was practically shaking.

"Which one is he?" Troy asked.

Her friend beamed, "He's in the black. Tall, mysterious, handsome."

"Oh, I've seen him around before. Mr. Player."

"He isn't!" Beatrice defended.

Troy laughed. "He's had three girlfriends already this year."

"You're just mad because one of them was a girl you liked," Marie said, grinning but also kicking Troy hard under the table as if to warn him not to cockblock their friend. "He's dreamy. Beatrice, go talk to him!"

Beatrice shook her head and laughed. "No way."

"What's there to be afraid of? He's cute." Beatrice didn't look convinced, so she pressed harder. "You know, I heard he was asking about you."

Beatrice's eyes grew wide, "Really?"

Marie nodded with a smile, "He just might be as nervous as you."

"Doubt it," Troy said under his breath.

"I'll kill you! Stop it!" Marie threw tortilla chips at the boy and groaned. "Don't listen to that party pooper. He's just angry because he's forever alone. Seriously, Beatrice, I say this because I care . . . go get you some!" The table erupted into laughter.

"Ugh, *fine*! I should just do it. Just say hi. I can pretend to bump into him or something."

"Just act natural," Marie said matter-of-factly.

Beatrice sat up straight and nodded. "Okay. Here I go."

"Oh, she looks so awkward," Marie giggled. "Poor, sweet thing."

Alex turned around and watched her. She did move a little awkwardly, Alex smiled.

The boy in black was very tall and very muscular, Alex noticed, studying him. He had a Tom Cruise smile and confidence Alex could feel all the way from where he sat.

"Who's he?" Alex asked.

"Ian," Troy answered.

The girl took a bite of her enchiladas. "She's been fawning over him for weeks. She's pretty much in love with him. You should see her binders."

Troy laughed. "Did she write all over them?"

Marie nodded. "I saw her doodling in math. At our sleepover last week, she couldn't stop talking about him. I guess they had a little encounter in the hall and he said she was cute! Which, of course, she is."

The Ian character seemed genuinely happy talking to Beatrice, Alex noted, and she, too, was lit up like fireworks as she spoke.

"I hope they get together!" Her friend rubbed her two index fingers together and made kissing noises.

Alex felt uncomfortable at the thought.

"Has she dated anyone before?" Troy asked.

The girl shrugged, "I don't think so. Alex, do you know if she has?"

Alex shook his head and turned away from the unsettling scene of Beatrice and that Ian guy, but the image of her drooling over that man never left his mind. He didn't feel like eating anymore.

"Isn't she just so innocent?" Marie grinned, clasping her hands together and watching the couple with wonder in her eyes.

"Thank you for coming out here." Beatrice took Rex off the leash and smiled at the lab as he took his first steps of freedom. "It's always nice to have someone with me."

The boy nodded.

It had been a few days since they had last seen each other due to the holiday break, and he had missed her.

It was Sunday morning, just hours after the rain. The earth was damp and the air deliciously fresh. Beatrice took a deep breath, inhaling the lingering smell of rain. This was her favorite weather during her favorite time of day. She looked to Alex and reconsidered. Perhaps her favorite time of day was late afternoon, around seven o'clock up until sunset.

"How are the parents?" She asked.

"They're good. They're the same: my mom always over the moon and my dad trying to balance it out."

"I always liked your mom. Your dad, too, of course, but your mom and I got along so well."

"She loved you." Alex smiled to himself, staring at his shoes and remembering his mother asking about Beatrice nearly every day.

"How is Beatrice?" His mother had asked for perhaps the third time that week.

"I don't know. She moved. Remember?"

"You should have kept in contact with her. She was so lovely."

The boy grimaced. "Well, it's too late for that."

"Maybe not. You never know what lies ahead."

HIS MOTHER WOULD MARRY THE TWO OF THEM IF SHE COULD, Alex thought.

Beatrice smiled, "Good."

"What about your dad? How is he?"

She laughed, "Trying way too hard. Poor guy, he's trying to compensate. He's good, though."

"Your friends seem to suit you."

"Do they?" The girl chuckled.

"They're a little weird, like you."

"I like them. I think they suit me, too."

Alex fell back and studied the girl. She began to hum, but it was quiet, nearly nonexistent and an almost lonely tune. And though she seemed to dance with each step, there was something offbeat about her movements that Alex just couldn't pinpoint.

"How are you?" He peered. "How is your life?"

She was surprised by the question. "All right. It's life, you know? It has its ups and downs."

"But you're happy?"

Beatrice glared at her feet, wondering why he cared so much. "As much as a seventeen-year old can be. But I have been seeing this guy lately. It's been really great." She looked down at her feet and blushed. "He's really sweet. Maybe things are going well, I don't know, uh, life is strange right about now. Isn't it?"

"I suppose." He couldn't quite agree with her. His life was perfectly normal—to his own standards at least. The girl was the only strange aspect, and that's how it had always been.

"What about your life?"

"Fine as usual."

"As usual," she rolled her eyes. "Aka: you haven't done anything that would surprise me." Beatrice paused. "Have you fallen in love since I've been gone?"

The girl spun on her heels, her eyes as large and full of wonder and mischief just as he had always known. Her lips stretched into a smile so slow it caught his breath as it formed.

But love? That was an idea he never believed he would entertain, and now that he looked at her, really took in all she was, he found it nearly impossible to form a coherent answer. She exuded such duende and simultaneous tranquility and chaos, but now that Beatrice had grown, her chaos was less deadly and more enticing. Alex found her to be a terrifying thrill he yearned to experience.

"L-love?" he stammered.

The girl grinned.

"That's a silly concept."

She inched closer to him until she was but a breath away. "You look nervous." Beatrice soaked up the boy in that moment, gazing into his eyes and rediscovering him. "How innocent."

He could smell her shampoo and felt her breath on his skin. "W-we should g-go." He pushed past Beatrice, calling for Rex and struggling to hide that he was trembling. Even if it was Beatrice, a woman had never gotten so close to him before.

"So, what have you done since I've been away?"

"Uh, well, I've competed with robotics and concept design. My parents let me go to some camps. I went to Houston. I got to tour NASA which was incredible. I'm starting to run out of space in the garage. I mean, that's pretty much it. I haven't strayed from the ordinary."

"You know, it's really amazing that you've stuck with your passion all this time. I can't wait to see what you do in the future."

"So, what, are you saying you don't think science is quote super boring and just *bleh* end quote?"

"I never said that!"

Alex nodded. "You most certainly did."

"Well, I never sounded like your poor imitation of me, then."

They laughed and Alex said, "Fair enough."

The two settled in what they once called the Dark Woods, but it wasn't as daunting as the two remembered—at least not so early in the morning.

Rex plopped down, overjoyed to finally rest.

"Have you ever looked at the world and wondered why you exist? Why did you come to be in all of this?"

"Well, I believe in the Big Bang Theory, so I have contemplated this. It all began with—"

"I'm not meaning scientifically. Like how did your specific consciousness end up with you and why, how, were you important enough to exist right now in this very second?"

"Well, then, no, I guess I never have."

"Look." Beatrice rolled onto her stomach and pointed to the Earth. "Look at all the life in just six inches. Do you see the ants, the grass, the worm, and the soil?" Alex nodded and squinted to get a better look. "Why me, you know? Why do I exist?"

The boy didn't quite understand the question, or rather he didn't know what she wanted to hear. "Just the coincidence of particle formation."

"How unromantic." She groaned and pushed herself up.

"I don't know how you want me to answer."

"You've always been so serious. Where's your romanticism?"

"I've never been the romantic type. Besides, that view on life isn't entirely necessary."

The girl frowned and drove her finger into Alex's arm, poking the poor boy all over, "Do you mean to tell me that all this time you've let yourself remain snooty and just," Beatrice paused, a look of pity befalling her; she let out an exasperated sigh and pursed her lips, "stagnant?"

Stagnant.

Alex grew more furious the longer the word echoed. "Why is it that you want me to change?"

"It's not that I want you to change! I just . . . I-I . . . I only wish you'd let more people in."

The boy almost laughed. Was she being serious? "I'm fine the way I am. I'm not the problem. People are." He didn't want to be lectured about that, not by her, not by anyone.

"You don't have to be so alone, Alex. The world can be cruel at times, too cruel to face alone. But also, life can be so beautiful. Remember the swing? Our rocket experiment?" She groaned, "I don't know, I guess what I'm trying to say is, why would you want to experience those lovely moments alone?" She paused and if only for a moment, the girl felt ten million miles away from him. "What if I'm no longer around?"

She saw fear in his eyes. The air felt too heavy, she felt suffocated, so she spoke again but this time, with a smile. "Who will you have to take you on crazy adventures?"

"I wouldn't want to go with anyone else."

Beatrice smiled and took his hand. "My point is, I see you. I see how you see others. You immediately find the bad in them without giving them the chance. There are assholes, people like Brady Johnson, for example. However, I think people would surprise you if you watched them differently. Watch how their eyes light up when they speak about their passions. Watch how wide their smiles get when they see the person they love. I'd just hate for you to miss out on really wonderful experiences."

The boy forced a smile and patted her hand before slipping out of her grasp. She was right . . . a little . . . but it was also like getting a life lesson from one of the church ladies because they never ceased asking poor Alex why he didn't have a girlfriend yet.

Beatrice hated the look of discomfort on his face. Maybe she shouldn't have said anything at all, but it was needed. Right? But by who? Her or him? She didn't know.

She shook the thoughts away and grinned, "Plus, you're being selfish by keeping yourself from the world. People are missing out on your awesomeness."

Alex chuckled to himself, "Thanks. I'm sure they are."

The two watched in silence as the golden lab played with a rather daring butterfly.

The girl sighed as she stretched and snuggled into the nook of a tree. "Let's just stay here forever."

"Forever is a long time."

"I know." She patted the space next to her and Rex happily took the invitation. "It's just so peaceful here. No one here to hurt us."

"Not unless you get ahold of a stick," he teased. "You nearly broke my hand, remember?"

"Oh, geez. I don't think it was that serious. 'Tis but a scratch!"

"You're insane. You know that?"

"Shh, just come here."

And so he did. The three laid together under the protection of the tree, the distant rustling of leaves and songs of birds rocking them to sleep.

CHAPTER FOUR

Eccedentesiast
(n.) one who represses pain by stifling a smile

MUSIC SPILLED INTO THE LIVING ROOM FROM THE KITCHEN where Alex's mother and father were. His mother always listened to that big band swing, saxophone-and-dancing-shoes kind of jazz when she cooked. Frank Sinatra was the only man that could make her put on her cooking apron, she would always say.

Alex looked down at Rex. The lab rested his face on his paws and stared at the couple in the kitchen, wagging his tail. The golden fur in Rex's face was turning white, Alex observed. In fact, his face consisted mostly of white.

Wanting to join in the fun of the kitchen, Rex stood, his movements shaky as he staggered during the first few steps, but he found his momentum and proceeded forward with triumph. Alex hadn't noticed Rex's behavior as of late. When the boy thought of the dog, he always imagined the brilliant golden ball of excitement that ran around, but now that he pondered it, Rex was getting older.

"'L' is for the way you look at me!" Marianne's voice boomed from the other room, and Alex turned to watch.

She continued the song, setting down the spatula and pulling in her husband to join her. His father wasn't a big dancer. David despised the act, having the rhythm of a damp towel, but he never hesitated when his wife looked at him with those lovely green eyes.

"Take my heart, but please don't break it!" She couldn't sing, not very well, at least, and certainly not when she needed to belt a note, but that never stopped her. Alex smiled as the two twirled and dipped and spun in clumsy circles.

Winter Formal was soon, Alex thought, in just a couple weeks to be exact. He had never been to a dance before. Alex had very seldom gone to any school event if he wasn't forced.

His mother ran into the dining room table as she attempted an advanced spin, and the couple burst into laughter, Rex barking at the catastrophe.

It was his senior year, though, and his mother never missed an opportunity to tell him that if he ever wanted to try something new, this was his year to do it.

FOR THE PAST THREE DAYS, IT WAS AS IF ALEX HAD swallowed his tongue each time he was around Beatrice.

"What's wrong?" Beatrice asked, nudging the boy with her shoulder.

"Nothing."

"Are you sure? You've looked completely stumped for days."

"I'm fine."

Beatrice didn't believe him, but if he insisted, then the case was closed. She didn't know how to get information out of him. She had always been on the other side of his closed door, but one day she'd change that.

"He asked me! Can you believe it?" a girl squealed, hugging tight to a bouquet of flowers.

Her friend cheered, "About time!"

Alex felt his palms sweat at the thought of Winter Formal. He stole a glance at Beatrice, his nerves making him feel queasy.

"I can't believe you won't be coming to see the show," she pouted, "but, then again, I'm missing your competition."

"I wouldn't expect you to see mine. It's in another state, after all."

"I would try to, though! I've always wanted to go to Washington D.C. Besides, everyone knows the best seafood is on the east coast."

Beatrice was in the fall musical, but her shows were at the same time as Alex's national robotics competition. She had told him that if she wanted anyone besides her father to go, it was him, which made Alex leaving for Washington D.C. so much harder. The girl had told him everything about the musical. She told him she had a small role, which made her sad, but Alex discovered it wasn't a small role at all, just not the lead. "But there are no small roles," she had said, "only small actors." She would sing the songs for him sometimes, and her voice was extraordinary, leaps and bounds better than he had remembered. How she didn't land the lead astounded him.

They were in the parking lot, just a few spaces from Alex's humble car which Beatrice had forced him to name Holberry. She had gotten in the habit of walking him to his car after school before she raced off to rehearsal.

"Beatrice," he muttered, interrupting her.

"Yeah?"

"Wi-will you g-go to Winter Formal with me?" Alex felt light-headed and was certain he was moments away from vomiting.

The girl froze, and then exhaled slowly, her gaze falling onto Alex with what he could only categorize as pity, an expression which served only to make the boy's nausea more severe.

"I've already said yes to someone." She winced as she spoke, dreading the idea of her rejection causing him a single ounce of pain.

He took a deep breath. "I wish you'd reconsider."

"I'm so sorry, Alex, but I really like this guy! Thank you, though. It's very sweet of you to ask."

He scoffed, "Sweet?" The boy fished out his keys and walked to his car alone. "Have a good day at rehearsal."

ALEX HAD AVOIDED BEATRICE FOR THE REST OF THE WEEK, though he couldn't stop thinking about his proposal. He was surprised by how much her response had affected him. In fact, he didn't know how much he had wanted to go with Beatrice until she turned him down. Maybe he should have asked her sooner . . .

Avoiding Beatrice didn't make much of a difference because she was hardly around anymore. Beatrice's free time was spent with Ian, the tall, muscular, and handsome boy she was quickly falling in love with. Perhaps too quickly, but all teenage girls fall blindly in love with sweet words and sparkling eyes.

The boy sat across from his parents having dinner at a restaurant, frowning as he messed with the napkin on his lap.

He didn't like thinking about her and *Ian*.

"What are you getting to eat, honey?" His mother smiled at her son.

Alex looked back at the menu. "I don't know yet." He would probably get the same thing he always got, something simple, something safe.

"Well, chicken is off the menu for you tonight, I can tell you that right now. I don't want to hear you ordering any chicken strips. You're almost an adult. Order something new!"

"What about the bacon pineapple burger, son? That's what I'm getting," his father offered.

"He's never liked anything sweet on his food, honey."

"Which is a sin! Besides, you said he should try something new."

Marianne pursed her lips and glared at the menu before grinning at the tired teenage boy across the table. "Your father's right. Why don't you get that? The pineapple actually tastes pretty good!"

Alex sighed; the chicken strips with barbecue sauce had been calling his name. "We'll see."

The boy leaned back in his seat and stretched, his eyes falling on the door just as a father and daughter strode in.

Beatrice.

His eyes grew wide in shock and his arms shot down to his lap instantly, but it was too late.

Beatrice had spotted him, and it had looked to her as if his stretch was a quick wave. The girl waved back and smiled.

"Who's the cutie?" his mother whispered over the table.

"Oh, leave him alone!" his father chortled, taking a sip of his beer.

"It's, uh, Beatrice."

"Oh! I can't believe it! They must eat with us! Darling, get the waiter to bring us an extra chair."

"Mom, please don't," Alex muttered, wishing they had picked another restaurant.

"Honey, let them eat in peace—,"

"David, another chair." She growled at her husband, checking her teeth in her pocket mirror before gliding to Beatrice and her father.

Alex felt sick to his stomach as Beatrice took the seat next to him. It was bad enough that she had shot him down, but the fact that he hadn't responded to her last several texts made the encounter much more uncomfortable for the boy.

"You're still alive," she whispered to him. "I thought maybe something had happened."

"Sorry."

Marianne grinned. "It's so great to see you both! How long has it been?"

"Five years." Beatrice smiled, taking the menu from the waiter.

"Wow! I can hardly believe it. Well, you've certainly grown into a beautiful young woman."

"Thank you! And it's so nice being able to see you. Alex and I were just talking about you the other day."

His mother nudged him under the table with her foot. "Oh, really? I didn't know you were back in town! Alex, how long have you kept her from us?"

Alex shrugged.

"How have you been, John?"

"I've been well. We were able to get the same house, so that made the move back a lot easier."

"What luck! How'd you manage that?"

"Well, I never sold the house when we moved, I just put it

up for rent, and I'm glad I did. It just so happened that when the company transferred me back here, the renter's lease was up, so we snagged our home back."

"Glad to hear it. Well, you both are welcome over any time. We're having a barbecue this weekend . . ."

Alex's attention drifted in and out of the conversation. The four others at the table didn't seem to notice.

He tried his very best to keep a smile on his face to hide how horrible and uncomfortable he felt. It seemed Beatrice was doing the same, but the boy couldn't tell which of the pair was the more skilled eccendentesiast, unless, of course, he was the only one shook by their last encounter.

Stop thinking about it, Alex told himself, squirming in his seat.

The boy's hand was in his lap, clenched in a fist, and Beatrice took hold of it, giving him a reassuring squeeze. The girl smiled gingerly, the boy hopelessly locked into her gaze.

She whispered, "I'm sorry." She let go of his hand, not wanting to overdo it. "I'm happy to run into you, though."

"Me, too," he stammered.

"Are you actually?" Beatrice chuckled as if she didn't believe him and rejoined the table's conversation.

CHAPTER FIVE

lexithymia
(n.) the difficulty in experiencing, expressing, and describing emotional responses

IT WAS SILLY. ALEX HAD BEEN TELLING HIMSELF THAT FOR hours, days even, yet there he sat on his bed staring at the tuxedo hanging on his closet door. The tuxedo mocked him, but it wasn't the clothes that snickered, rather the idea that they represented. He didn't belong at an event like Winter Formal, especially not if it was all to go after an unrequited feeling. He wasn't that kind of romantic hero, and he never wanted to be. Nevertheless, Alex couldn't get her out of his mind.

Rex's tail thumped against the bed frame, drawing the boy's attention. When Alex looked down at the dog, all he could hear was Rex screaming at him, *Go! Do it, you idiot!*

And Alex was right; however, Rex wasn't thinking about his owner racing off to some dance. Instead, the dog was thinking more along the lines of: *Go! Get me a treat!* or *Go! Take me outside* or *Pet me for God's sake, you idiot!*

There was a knock on his door . . . again . . . and sure enough it was his mother as it had been the past ten times.

"Are you sure you don't need any help?" she called through the door. "Oh! Maybe you want to use your father's cologne?"

Alex grumbled. "I'm not going."

"Don't be silly, honey. This will be a great opportunity for you."

"Let him be," his father called from the other room. "If he wants to wallow in self-pity and is fine with being alone—,"

"David! Don't you dare say that!"

His father grumbled low, "It's true."

Marianne knocked lightly on the door once more, but this time stepped inside. "Sweetie, don't listen to your father. He's just a grumpy old man." Alex laughed, relieving his poor mother. "What's keeping you?"

"It's nothing."

She didn't believe him for a second. Marianne sighed, "I respect you and your decisions. You know that, right?" The boy nodded. "I think you're very smart. You have a good head on your shoulders and a good heart. I couldn't be prouder of the man you're becoming. Just don't be afraid to take risks, too."

She patted her son's leg and went to leave.

"Mom," Alex called. She stopped and faced her son. "Thank you."

"Of course," she smiled. "Oh, and if you don't go tonight, I'll have to take away your computer for a week." Marianne winked as she closed his door behind her.

"What?" he shouted, his heart racing at the very idea.

Her laughter filled the house, "You heard me!"

Alex sighed and redirected his attention to the tuxedo as he rested his hand on the dog's head, rubbing just behind the ear.

"Why don't we climb it?" Beatrice had said so long ago. The girl had been standing beneath the largest tree Alex had ever seen. The branches had hung low and so thick that Alex could hardly find it within himself to call them branches instead of more trees.

"I don't think so," he gulped.

"Scaredy cat! Come on, you'll love it!" She had leapt to the first branch and held out her hand, flashing the boy a smile so calm and reassuring that he couldn't resist.

Beatrice never lost that smile, Alex thought. In fact, she perfected it, if that was possible, and he found comfort in that constant.

And as he recalled the first time he saw her since those five years, that slow as molasses moment in the hallway, one sentence came to mind:

"I just might marry you, Mr. Holberry."

With those words echoing, Alex tore the tuxedo from the door.

It was a suffocating feeling fighting through the sea of people, and the blasting music threatened to give him a migraine.

He gritted his teeth and continued searching, constantly pulling at his tuxedo. It was a cheap rental and the boy hadn't bothered getting it fitted.

She was nowhere to be found and Alex became conscious of more and more people taking notice of him as he started passing by the same tables multiple times in his search. As time waned on, the stares felt like a thousand pricks and he began to feel uncomfortably hot, even without the tuxedo jacket.

"Stupid," he muttered under his breath as the boy stepped outside and leaned against the building. A cold breeze blew past him. He fiddled with the car keys in his pocket. Alex simply wasn't the kind of person who could sweep a girl off her feet, and he had always known and accepted that. He shouldn't have come, Alex thought, growing angry with himself.

A loud cheer disturbed the silence.

"Shh! Come on, dude!"

Curious, Alex crept around the corner, spying on a group hiding in the courtyard.

"No one's out here to see us. Relax, man." One of the boys rested against a wall with his hands behind his back.

"If we get caught out here, I'm kicking your ass!" A tall boy growled, towering over the other. Alex's eyes grew wide and he turned to leave, not wanting any part in what was going on.

"Chill out, guys," her voice was honey-sweet and slow.

Alex stopped.

Beatrice.

Glancing back, he watched the girl appear from behind the massive figure of the taller boy. She wore red and moved so slowly, so gracefully, that it looked like she was underwater. Alex's lips stretched into a bright grin and he strode to her without thinking.

"Incoming," one of the other girls muttered as she caught sight of the boy.

The others hid small bags, pipes, and pill bottles in their pockets with ferocious speed.

"Alex!" Beatrice grinned and glided to the boy, over-joyed by the sight of him.

"I was looking everywhere for you," Alex said as Beatrice fell into his arms, giggling.

"I can't believe you came! Do you have a date?" Beatrice's face was buried in his neck as she held onto him.

"N-no, I actually came for you." He felt anxious and considered not telling her at all.

She pulled away from Alex and smiled.

"I just wanted to-to, um..."

Beatrice tried hard to listen to him. She stood uncomfortably straight and stared at his mouth to help herself make out the words. A memory crept forward of Alex accidentally dropping popsicle juice on his chin, so most of her concentration went into her trying not to laugh at the thought.

She wanted to lay down. God, did she feel good! She felt good and relaxed, she thought with a wide smile.

"Beatrice," Alex said for the second time, growing intensely impatient.

Her eyes traveled to his and she smiled, "Yes?"

The boy glared at her, his scowl transforming into disbelief. "Are you high?"

Beatrice's eyes grew wide and jaw dropped in horror. "No!"

"Who the hell is this guy?" It was the tall one who spoke, putting his arm around Beatrice and glaring down at the boy. Alex recognized the figure as the light shone on his face. It was Ian, Beatrice's crush.

So, *he* was her date. Alex grimaced.

Alex ignored him and studied Beatrice. Her eyes were glossy and she didn't seem entirely there. "What's going on?" His attention shifted from the girl to those around her. He didn't feel right about it.

"Nothing," the tall one, Ian, answered. "You should go."

"You're right," Alex took hold of Beatrice's hand, "Come on, we're leaving."

Beatrice was too surprised to do anything but follow Alex.

"The hell do you think you're doing?" Ian wrenched Beatrice back, making her cry out and stumble.

He was nothing like the boy Alex remembered in the restaurant, nor anything like the guy Beatrice had described him to be.

Beatrice held her arm and glared at the ground, feeling far too out-of-body to be able to react.

"Don't grab her like that." Alex tightened his fist. "And keep her out of whatever you're doing. Beatrice, let's go." He held his hand out for her, but she only stared at it wide-eyed.

"What did I just say?" Ian grabbed Alex's collar.

"J-just let us l-leave."

"She isn't going anywhere, but you are." Ian threw Alex to the side, and then turned swiftly and grabbed Beatrice's arm. "You can't just invite people like this. The hell do you think you're doing?" He whispered something in her ear, his expression deepening into something darker by the second, and then pushed her away, muttering, "You're more trouble than you're worth."

It was the look of absolute shock and agony on Beatrice's face that set Alex's blood on fire.

Alex only saw red.

He tackled Ian. Alex drove his fists into him, bloodying his knuckles.

Ian laughed, kicking Alex off him and delivering punches of his own.

Alex's head slammed against the concrete, making him too dizzy to move.

He lay there. The blurry figure of Ian leapt over him and knocked the air out of his lungs.

Alex's head fell to the side. As his vision returned, he saw Beatrice. She was being held back by one of the others. She looked so feeble as she wailed, struggling to break free.

Letting out a cry, Alex rammed his head into the boy, sending him reeling back. Alex swung at Ian with all the strength he had and kicked him square in the chest. Ian fell over a bench, his head thudding against a brick.

Ian didn't move, and Alex stood over him, shaking with rage and feeling the overwhelming sensation of both power and fear.

Ian's friends rushed to the scene, pushing past Alex and dropping Beatrice.

"He's breathing!" one shouted.

"Oh, thank God, he's fine!"

One turned and burned a hole into Alex, "You bastard. I'm—"

"Sorry, guys!" Beatrice sang, taking hold of Alex's hand. "We gotta go!"

The boy and girl bolted, a blur of red and black as they raced to the school parking lot.

Far from the danger behind them, Beatrice stopped, collapsing on the hood of a car. "I-I can't run any . . . anymore," she whispered.

"Let's just get to my car,"

"The metal feels good." The girl grinned, fanning out on the hood as if she were making snow angels. "I feel *so* hot and this feels *so* cool."

"This isn't either of our cars, Beatrice. Let's go."

"Let's just stay here forever." She pointed to the sky. "Do you think that's the North Star?"

Alex followed her gaze, "I don't think so. It's not very bright."

"Count the stars with me," she cooed, pulling at the boy's arm with a sugar-sweet smile.

Alex felt paranoid and couldn't stop glancing back at the school. Getting beat up in a parking lot wasn't his plan for the night—getting into a fight at all wasn't in the cards. "How about we count them somewhere else?" Beatrice pouted and turned from him. "We can go to a park. Wouldn't you like to count them at a park?" She nodded slowly and rolled back over, still on the hood of a stranger's car. Alex smiled. "I'll even get you some candy at the store."

***

ALEX STOLE A GLANCE AT THE GIRL. SHE LAID ON THE GRASS with a bottle of water balancing upright on her stomach, a pack of M&M's in her hand, and a smile glued to her face. She had been staring at the sky for twenty minutes and doing nothing but plopping candy into her mouth or softly giggling every so often.

Alex frowned, studying the sky with her. There were hardly any stars.

Beatrice whispered, "The water bottle feels like an elephant on my stomach."

"Then take it off."

She shook her head no, and then giggled to herself.

He had planned on saying so much when he found her. Alex wanted to tell her about the first time he saw her, both back when they first met and when he saw her in the hallway. He had worked up the courage to tell her just how beautiful she was. As he looked at her now—yes, still beautiful in the deep red dress and lovely curls splayed out around her like a crown as she beamed under the moon—she was a mess, and he felt trapped in alexmythia. He didn't know what she was on, what she had taken or smoked, and he wasn't sure if she would remember what happened. Hell, he had to carry her off the hood of the stranger's car and to his own because she swore to him that her legs were jellyfish. Alex didn't understand what that meant.

Alex redirected his attention to his feet where his cup of coffee sat. He wasn't sure how long they would be at this park, but Alex didn't plan on returning Beatrice home while she was high as a kite.

"I feel funny. Do you feel funny, Mr. Holberry?"

"No, I don't."

She hummed and held up her hands, playing imaginary piano above her. "I like it."

"What is it?"

"What is what?"

"What you're on."

Beatrice grinned and began playing piano on Alex's leg. "I don't remember. I think it starts with an 'o.' You look nice. I like you all dressed up."

"Thank you." Alex ran his fingers through his hair and sighed. "I'd feel a lot better if you didn't hang out with those people again."

Beatrice's fingers halted and she stared at Alex. She didn't like the look on his face, for he looked disappointed in her and that was the last thing she wanted. Sighing, her eyes fell to the grass. The blades swirled beneath her, dancing, though there was no wind.

The world became very loud for the girl, and yet so painfully quiet all at once. "He said I . . . he said I was lousy."

"Lousy?" The boy almost laughed. Who said "lousy" anymore? "Who? That boy?"

She nodded slowly, her head feeling light as a feather, yet her thoughts dragging her terribly low. "A lousy, lousy lay."

Beatrice would never forget those words.

Alex didn't know what to say, but, God, did he want to kill the bastard. His fists tightened, the whites of his knuckles nearly breaking through. She rested her hand on his, and her warmth calmed him.

The girl then touched his jaw, tracing the beginnings of a bruise. "Does it hurt?"

He let out a short laugh and lied, "Not at all."

"You're so strong."

"I don't know about that."

"You are. You stood up for me. I wanted to help."

"It's fine. I don't blame you. Your legs are jellyfish, remember?" she giggled. "I just don't see why you got yourself into that mess."

"You've never stood up for me before."

"I'm sorry about that. I-I never . . ." He trailed off, feeling flustered and anxious.

Beatrice waited for him to finish, watching him in a dreamy haze.

"You've changed," she said, her lips stretching into a smile that seemed to scream, *Finally!*

"It's nothing. I just—"

She kissed him.

Alex didn't move, or couldn't move, he didn't know, but, God, her lips were soft and tasted like chocolate.

CHAPTER SIX

A	traxia
	(n.) a state of freedom from emotional distur-
	bance and anxiety; tranquility

"Forget her? Move on? You say it like the act is so simple." Beatrice stood tall with her hands balled into fists so tight Alex feared their damage. "Have you ever lost someone? Have you ever stayed up every night with every breath burning from hours of crying? Have you ever felt a part of you die? It's agonizing, so don't you dare tell me to move on. She was my everything, the one thing that gave me the strength to wake up in the morning. If I can do anything to avenge her, I will!" Her lips curled into a dangerous smile. "And I can. Don't you see? I know who did it. I have all the pieces! When I find him, I'll kill him! I'll rip him limb from limb and burn the remains. No! Don't you try to stop me! I swear I'll do the same to anyone who dares get in my way." She collapsed, staring at her shaking hands as soft sobs wracked her body, and then she looked to him, broken and hopeless with a voice as gentle as a whisper. "She . . . she's gone. Don't you understand? That's all I can do."

The forest was silent and Alex frozen.

"End scene!" Beatrice leapt to her feet and grinned.

"Wow," he breathed, still awestruck by the girl.

"I hope I do well."

"If you audition like that, they'll give you whatever part you want."

Beatrice laughed, digging her hands deep into her coat pockets and stepping gingerly on to a thin sheet of ice that decorated the woodsy path. The ice cracked and shattered and she frowned. "I don't know. The other girls are prettier and parents richer. You may say different, but truthfully, that always wins in the end."

"But you have the talent."

"I hope so."

Alex sighed. "You have a strange way of being irritatingly optimistic, and then the next moment you paint the world black."

She shrugged. "That's the mystery of me, I guess."

Beatrice paraded in front of him, leading him onward with slow, long strides. She played music as they ventured. It was slow and soft, a perfect blend for the winter around them. And as the minutes sank into an hour, Alex saw Beatrice melt into quiet melancholy.

Rex laid down on a patch of dried leaves within Lorial Pass, and Beatrice, finding it to be a good spot, joined her trusted Regenald.

The boy sat back as she ran her fingers through the lab's golden fur.

Weeks had passed, yet the feel of her lips had never left his. They hadn't spoken about the kiss. For all Alex knew, the girl didn't remember.

Beatrice didn't want to remember. She felt mortified and if she could've forgotten the entire night, she would've. She wanted to forget so much of her life. The girl simply didn't feel like herself; even in the forest, within the domain of the great King Beatrice, she was a stranger. Beatrice sighed and scratched Rex behind his ear.

She had been changing. Her friends may not have seen it, but Alex certainly could. The forest was the only place she came alive anymore, he noted—the forest and the stage, anyway. There was something deep within her that wasn't the same. It was her laugh or her smile or the way she walked. Whatever it was, Alex sensed her atraxia slipping away.

But he couldn't find the words to ask.

Regenald Rex's fur was chilled. Beatrice frowned, "He's cold."

"We should probably head back."

The girl nodded and walked in Alex's footprints.

Beatrice's hand lingered on an icy branch, her fingers burning from the cold, yet hesitant to retract. "Have you heard of Yuki Onna?"

"Who?"

"Yuki Onna. The Snow Woman."

Alex shook his head *no*.

"There are tales of her in Japan. Most see her as a tall woman, beautifully pale with long, onyx black hair, and a thin, white kimono. She comes during snow storms, like a vision amidst the white. And, though both stunning and ageless, her skin can give a man an unshakeable chill, so when a traveler draws near, she takes their warmth."

Alex laughed, "Are you sure you're not talking about Rogue from *X-Men*? She doesn't have ice powers, but it's close. Oh, or maybe that one guy from *Smallville* . . . God, what was his name?"

A frigid gust of wind hit as Alex turned to face Beatrice. Her curls blew in her face, though her eyes were visible and deadly. "Yuki Onna isn't always dangerous. Sometimes she falls in love. But mostly," the boy felt undeniable fear as she marched towards him, the sky growing dark and wind hollowing as she reached her bare fingers to his cheek, "she kills."

His heart jumped to his throat. Though she had been dormant for so long, Beatrice was a frightening thing when she wanted to be. "Are you going to kill me?"

"Perhaps," she whispered and lead Rex away.

With a snack in hand, Alex waited at the bottom of the staircase, spying on his parents. It was Friday night and that meant it was their drinking and *Whose Line Is It Anyway?* night. The couple sat in each other's laps with their eyes glued to the television and glass of liquor in hand. Alex liked watching at times like that, when they were so in love, especially when his father burst into uncontrollable laughter.

Smiling, the boy shook his head and trekked up the stairs, but tired Rex stayed behind.

He sat on his bed and looked about his room with a glum expression. Posters from science magazines, certificates, and awards hung neatly spaced throughout his walls and he had bookshelves upon bookshelves filled with books and papers written by his heroes. He frowned, displeased by the mess on the floor. *I should probably tidy up*, he thought. But the more pressing concern was that Alex was less than thrilled that he'd be returning to school in just a few days. His holiday break had been blissfully lazy, aside from Beatrice dragging him out of the house every now and again, which he didn't really mind.

Alex's gaze landed on a small device on his bedside table. He lifted it and studied the object with a careful eye. It was a diptych sundial that Beatrice had gifted him on Christmas when she told him it was so he could navigate more efficiently as Mr. Holberry. The girl had laughed when she said it, but Alex had an inkling that she was serious; they hadn't played in ages, but he knew she missed it.

He ran his thumb over the smooth box, reading over the cities listed on the top: Athenas, Berlin, Danczig, Venetia, etc. Opening it, he traced over the painted flowers which looked dated enough to be from the 17th century. The bright blue hand on the dial spun and twirled about as he fiddled with the trinket. The sundial was unnecessary and silly, but the boy still found odd comfort in it.

Alex's phone vibrated in his pocket.

"Hello?" he answered, surprised that Beatrice would call so late at night.

Loud music and muffled voices boomed in the background.

"Alex!" she sang.

"I can barely hear you. Where are you?" He frowned. Alex wasn't pleased with the idea of her partying, not after Winter Formal.

The boy heard a door closing through the phone and the background noise grew faint.

"It's so boring here, Alex," she moaned.

"Doesn't sound like it. Do you need anything?"

"I don't like these people."

"Beatrice, are you okay?"

"I saw Ian here."

Alex's blood boiled and he nearly snapped his phone in

half from the tightness of his grip. "Is he still there? Has he hurt you? Did you take anything from him?"

"No, I-I hid until he left."

"That's good. I don't think you should be around him."

"I've been avoiding him at," she hiccupped, "at school."

"I've been, too, honestly. But, hey, are you okay?"

"My friend invited me and I don't know where she went."

"Are you—"

"It's weird here," she interjected. "I don't know. Come keep me company!"

Alex sighed, "Can you send me the address?" Her answer was muffled. "Beatrice?"

Silence.

"Yeah?"

"Can you send me the address? Do you know where you are?"

There was no noise on the girl's end. Anxiety crept upon the boy.

"Umm, yes. I can get it. Bye."

The girl hung up.

He threw on a jacket, grabbing an extra just in case, and went downstairs. "I'll be back later. I'm going to pick up Beatrice."

"But it's so late!" his mother called, her head peeking out from behind the couch. And she was right; it was midnight.

"Yeah, I know. I'll be careful."

"Let us know if you need anything." His father smiled at him.

Alex sat in his car for what felt like an eternity, drumming his thumbs against the steering wheel as he awaited her text. Maybe he should call her back, he thought, but then his phone buzzed.

4810 Atterson Road

Twenty-three miles away, Alex groaned.

Be safe until I get there, he texted back.

The house was on the outskirts of the city, and the street it was on was packed with cars.

Putting on a brave face, Alex marched inside. He, like Beatrice, didn't recognize anyone at the party.

"Excuse me, do you know Beatrice?"

"What?" a guy shouted, spilling some of his beer on Alex's shoe. "Sorry, bro!"

"Do you know Beatrice?" he asked again and much louder. The boy shook his head no. "She's a little shorter than me with curly hair."

"Sorry, dude."

Alex kept searching. No one had heard of her, and when he mentioned the curly hair, he was continuously sent to the same girl who looked nothing like Beatrice.

The boy was beginning to lose hope. She wasn't answering his phone calls or texts and he was starting to think the address was wrong.

A sense of dread sat heavy in his stomach as he opened a door on the second floor of the home. If she wasn't in that last room, she wasn't at the house, Alex decided.

A body was draped facedown across the bed.

The boy's heart stopped.

Dear God, he thought, *please don't let that be her*.

Alex ran to the girl, carefully turning her over.

It was Beatrice.

Small pools of vomit had sunk into the bed around her and remains of the bile coated her lips and chin.

Don't let this be real, the boy prayed. *Please, don't let this be real!*

"Beatrice, wake up." Alex was shaking as he wiped the vomit away and checked her pulse. He waited, but his hands were too unsteady to tell if he felt her blood pulsing or his own fingers trembling.

"Come on, please say something. Can you hear me? Groan, open your eyes. Jesus, Beatrice, do anything!"

Alex opened one of her eyes. Her pupils were unnaturally narrow.

The boy felt sick as he pulled out his phone and dialed an ambulance.

He lifted her as carefully as he could manage and carried her to the bathroom. Alex dampened a cloth and put it on the back of her neck as he spoke to her, praying that his voice might bring her back.

As more time passed and she remained as still as before, Alex lost all composure.

"Beatrice, please," he cried, bringing her to his chest. "Don't leave me, please. Don't be gone, oh, God, please don't leave me." He checked her pulse again and again, but couldn't hold himself steady enough to get a reading.

Sirens wailed over the music and the boy heard the shouting of frantic teenagers as they bolted from the scene. Alex carried her in his arms down the stairs, his eyes never leaving the sweet face of the girl whose life meant more to him than his own. His steps were shaky and he nearly fell, barely strong enough to carry her.

Her face was so pale and lifeless, losing more color with every step the boy took.

He was too late.

He hadn't made it in time.

He had failed her.

Everyone stopped and watched in absolute shock and guilt as EMTs burst into the house and took Beatrice from Alex's arms and sat her on the gurney.

"What can you tell us?" one asked.

"I-I don't know. I drove here and f-found her passed out in her own vomit. Her pupils a-are so small and sh-she feels cold. I can . . . I can barely check her pulse."

"Had she been drinking tonight?" another questioned as they carried her to the ambulance.

"I-I don't know. I just got here. Sh-she could have been."

"So, you don't know if she had been taking any drugs either, do you?"

"M-maybe. I'm not sure."

They loaded the girl into the ambulance, but stopped Alex as he climbed in.

He didn't take his eyes off Beatrice. "Please, let me ride with you."

"No can do, son." The EMT looked at him with sad eyes.

"She's coming back!" one called from inside the ambulance.

Alex's knees gave way underneath him.

"We need to get her to the hospital!"

The boy lurched forward towards the vehicle. As the paramedic pushed him down and onto the concrete, he screamed her name, her sweet, sweet name. *Beatrice!*

The doors shut, and as the ambulance sped away, leaving the boy alone on the ice-cold pavement, Alex felt as though his whole life had been ripped away.

CHAPTER SEVEN

M ellifluous
(adj.) sweetly or smoothly flowing; sweet sounding

THE AIR OF THE HOSPITAL HALLWAY WAS THICK WITH WORDS left unspoken.

Beatrice's father, John, sat two seats away from Alex, his head bent, back hunched, and hands clasped. Seeing the girl lie in the hospital bed was hauntingly akin to seeing his wife in the same place all those years ago. It never stopped hurting. And if he ever believed that pain could never rip him apart more than that day he lost his wife, he was so very wrong. He had failed her once again. He had failed his wife and he had failed his precious Bee.

Alex felt numb. The feeling of believing her dead for even a minute lingered with him. If he had arrived ten minutes later than he had, perhaps she wouldn't have been so lucky.

Ten minutes, he thought.

Ten stupid minutes.

The thought sickened him.

"John, is it?" the doctor asked after the door closed behind her.

The father nodded and stood, following the doctor down the hall and out of Alex's earshot.

"She is alive and awake."

"Oh, thank God."

The doctor looked to John with a pained expression; this was always the worst part of her day. "We found heavy traces of OxyContin. The levels would have been enough to kill her had she not come in when she did, especially since the drug was paired with quite a bit of alcohol. Unfortunately, that was not all we found. Rohypnol was also discovered. She has no memory of taking the substance and was found unconscious. That may have been due to the opioid, but nevertheless, as it is the," her words came out shaky, "date-rape drug, it is cause for concern."

John felt lightheaded and leaned against the wall to keep upright. His sweet, precious child. . .

"Once she has rested, we will undergo a few tests to ensure she wasn't sexually assaulted. But overall, the good news is that your daughter is breathing and recovering."

"Thank you." John could hardly speak, least of all think. His little girl. . .

"Now, I do have some questions for you. Has your daughter shown any signs of being suicidal?"

The two spoke for a while longer, by which time Alex had stopped watching and redirected his attention to the ground at his feet.

John was allowed into the room; the doctor having said immediate family only for the time being. The man stopped, his hand clutching the door handle. Her father exhaled slowly and glared at the door. "I can't thank you enough for what you did for my daughter." John's gaze fell on Alex, a boy who had become something of a son to him in the past few months. "I can't lose her."

"I know, sir."

"No. No, you don't, and I hope you never will."

He disappeared beyond the door, leaving Alex in the hall.

The boy's head fell between his knees. He didn't know what to think or how to react and, react to what exactly? What happened? What did the doctor tell John? There were too many questions, and though she was maybe fifteen feet from him, with just one hospital room wall between them, he felt a million miles away.

"Alex!" His mother's voice shook the hallway as she ran towards her son with a plate in her hands. Even his father was rushing at full speed, yet still dragging behind the frantic woman.

The boy hadn't wanted to tell his parents. In fact, he was in such a shock that when his mother called, desperate to find out where her son was, he didn't notice. It took twenty messages and two missed calls for the boy to feel his phone buzz in his pocket.

"Where is she?" Marianne asked, completely out of breath as she held the plate wrapped in foil for dear life.

Alex pointed to the room in front of him.

"Is she okay? What happened?"

"I-I don't know. I don't know anything." Alex ran his fingers through his hair and sighed. He just wanted to know what happened. No, he just needed to know that she was going to be okay.

His mother fell into a seat. "Oh, God."

Alex didn't know how much time had passed before John finally appeared in the doorway, but if someone had said it had been several hours or even days, he would have believed them.

John beckoned the boy into the room, but his mother pulled him aside first, saying, "Here. Take some of these for her." Marianne lifted the aluminum, exposing freshly-baked snickerdoodle cookies.

THE BOY WALKED INTO THE ROOM WITH HIS HEAD DOWN. John had left to get coffee while the girl slept, and the boy promised not to wake her. He sat near Beatrice, taking the chair John had moved closer to the bed so that he could hold his daughter's hand. Alex took a deep breath before he looked at her. He wasn't quite sure what he expected, but the image of her sunken face, pale and lifeless, haunted his thoughts.

Beatrice had regained some color since he last saw her. She looked healthy again, just like she was sleeping on any other ordinary night. But this was no ordinary night, the boy thought to himself as he moved a lock of hair away from her face.

Though he had been very reluctant, John had told the boy what the doctor said—OxyContin and Rohypnol, as if the first wasn't enough. Someone tried to drug her. *No. Someone did drug her. She was roofied.* Alex wiped away a tear and cleared his throat. He hadn't been there in time to protect her, and the fear of not knowing what happened while she was unconscious filled him with shame.

"Alex." Her voice was mellifluous, like a petal drifting just soft enough to land on water without disturbing its calm.

They stared at each other as minutes passed.

Looking her father and her truest friend—after what happened, how could he not be—in the eyes was more painful than she imagined. The girl felt ashamed and small, oh so very small and so, so incredibly stupid, because neither of the men were angry with her. They were simply sad.

"I-I'm so sorry," she whimpered, reaching for his hand.

"Please, it should be me apologizing. I should have been there sooner." The boy didn't just mean sooner that night. He was angry at himself for not being there for her sooner, for not breaking the silence and having a conversation when he first noticed the signs. He had failed her.

Beatrice hid her face under her arm as she fought back tears. She had never meant to cause such damage as she saw spelled out on his face, as she saw trembling on his lips, and as she felt in the quaking of his hands.

"C-can you just tell me why?" Alex gritted his teeth.

She sighed. "They think I was trying to commit suicide."

Her eyes were swollen and red, and cheeks just as worn and stained from tears. The girl, as she lay then in that lonely hospital bed, looked the opposite of the girl he knew and loved—she was no King Beatrice.

"Were you?"

"No. I'm not trying to kill myself. I'm just . . . I'm just trying to be happy."

The boy didn't know a whole lot about happiness; he would never call himself an expert on the topic. However, what he saw before him certainly didn't look like happiness.

She began to tear up. "I-I guess I haven't been doing a very good job."

As soon as Alex saw her first tear slip down her rosy cheeks, he buried his head in her chest and held her as if that embrace was the only thing keeping her alive.

CHAPTER EIGHT

S audade
(n.) a deep emotional state of melancholic longing
for a person or thing that is absent

It wasn't until the last day of winter break that Alex
was allowed to see Beatrice. It had been days since he had
seen her or even spoken to her. After the incident, her father
put her on lockdown and Alex had been pacing in his room
all that time, worried sick.

The two sat on the girl's porch, warmed from the steam of
hot chocolate.

Even with the time apart, Alex could formulate no words.
As soon as he saw her in the doorway, he became mute.

The girl knew why he was so quiet, why everyone was so
quiet around her lately; it was the same reason why everyone
from then on would have that same nervous and pitiful half-
smile to flash her, as if a word as little as hello would break
her. They were quiet because they knew. Everyone knew.
Even strangers—she could feel it every time she looked

someone in the eye. Everyone felt bad for her. Poor, helpless Beatrice. The paranoia that had set in during her time of isolation and constant doctor visits told her that to some degree, they all feared her as well.

She hated it.

The girl filled with more rage by the second.

Instinctually, Alex moved closer to Beatrice and wrapped an arm around her shoulder.

Her breathing slowed as she settled into a peaceful state. "Thank you for always keeping me grounded."

Alex responded with a smile and by ruffling up her curls.

She took a gulp of hot chocolate, going into full-on red alert mode as she spat it out, stuttering, "Hot! Hot! Hot!"

"Stupid," Alex chuckled.

Beatrice whimpered, "I forgot these were so hot."

"What am I going to do with you?"

The girl sighed, "It's the question everyone is asking themselves."

"Hey." Alex frowned and gently slapped the back of her head. "No one is thinking that. You aren't a burden to anyone."

Beatrice glared at the street ahead of them. "You're too good for me."

"Maybe," the boy teased. "But in some way, some weird and probably messed up way, we really fit together. Don't you think?"

She nodded and rested her head on his shoulder.

***

"Is Beatrice okay?"

Alex looked up from his desk to see a girl with worried eyes standing over him. The boy studied her. He had seen her before. His mind went back to the party and there she was: the blonde girl had been up against the kitchen counter, linked to a guy holding her waist and kissing her neck. Alex hadn't asked her about Beatrice that night, for the blonde girl and the guy hadn't looked like they'd be coming up for air anytime soon.

"I brought her to the party, and then she was being carried away by paramedics. What happened? She isn't texting me back."

"She's fine."

"Are you sure?" The girl with perfectly straight, blonde hair and far too much eye make-up knelt in front of him, resting her elbows on his desk and batting her big eyes. "I'm just really worried."

Alex hated her. He didn't know her but could see how ugly she was on the inside, the bitch. "I'm sure if you had taken better care of your friend, then you wouldn't have to be so worried."

But of course, that wasn't true; Alex was doing everything he could for Beatrice, but the guilt wasn't going away, and the worry only grew as days passed.

The girl rolled her eyes, "Whatever. Just tell her that she needs to text Hannah."

The bell rang and the girl sauntered out of the room.

Alex opened his textbook and began reading the assigned chapter, but, for once, his mind just wasn't on his studies. He planned to visit Beatrice after school. Honestly, he had half a mind to pack up and walk out that very second. Alex wanted to bring Rex as a surprise when he visited. The boy smiled at the thought of how happy it would make Beatrice, not to mention Rex.

His phone vibrated in his pocket.

MOM: ARE YOU ABLE TO TALK? IT'S IMPORTANT.

ALEX'S HEART DROPPED. THE ONLY THING HE COULD THINK of was Beatrice. Was she alive?

Alex's voice was soft as he tried not to echo in the hallway. "Hey, Mom, what's wrong?"

"Are you alone?"

"Yes, is everything okay?"

The boy felt nauseous from the anticipation.

"It's Rex. He was hit by a car while on a walk."

Alex froze and his phone crashed to the ground.

"Alex, honey, he isn't going to last much longer."

Everything in front of the boy was a blur and he hardly remembered grabbing his backpack or the drive to the vet.

His mother and father had their back to the door, shielding the sweet lab from sight when Alex stormed into the private room at the veterinarian's office. Alex screamed Rex's name, a frantic mess.

The lab moved his head to look in the direction of the boy, relishing the scent of Alex. He loved the boy, the boy that fell against the table and buried his head in his fur. And though the golden lab wasn't entirely sure what was happening or why everyone looked so sad or why he hurt so much, Rex had a feeling that he would never see that boy again.

"No! God, please!" the boy howled, holding to the lab with all his strength, crying into Rex's fur.

Rex had stopped breathing, his tail no longer wagged, and the blood was already beginning to dry.

Alex let out a cry as he punched the table, his father held him back, and doctors rushed to the dog.

"He's gone," the boy said through his gritted teeth. "Dammit, he's gone!"

"I know, son. I know."

IT JUST WASN'T THE SAME, BEATRICE THOUGHT.

Her gaze fell upon Alex. He held in one hand Rex's collar and in the other a ratted squirrel chew toy, Rex's favorite.

The two sat in King Beatrice's castle atop the growing bed of flower petals.

It just wasn't the same.

The glen was dark, Beatrice could feel no music, the petals were dead, and what flowers hadn't yet succumbed to the ice were withered. Even the air tasted sour and unforgiving.

They had chosen the castle as the burial ground, for it was where Rex seemed happiest. He had loved to roll in the petals amongst the butterflies and zoom around with an infectious fury.

And now he would never get that joy again.

Alex sat Rex's belongings on the ground, the first time he had let them go since the lab's body had been taken away. Alex's hands cut through the earth as he dug. The soil was cold and still slightly damp from the last snow. As the boy sat the relics in the bottom of the deep grave, he found he hadn't the strength to bury his lifelong friend. The soil sat ready, patient in his hands, yet he trembled, sending most of it to slip through his fingers and onto his jeans.

Beatrice cupped her hands around his, keeping a tiny morsel of soil from falling back to the earth. She looked at him slowly, unable to smile, unable to speak, but as their eyes met, words weren't needed. Sunlight broke through the trees behind her, and she was stunning, despite sorrow filling in her eyes. What would he had done, Alex thought, had he lost her, too? How could he have carried on?

The girl nodded and ever so slowly led Alex's hands over the small grave, where they let the soil cover what was left of Regenald Rex, their trusty wolf companion.

Is it not life's cruel joke to give irreplaceable joys that Death will surely reap?

The boy patted down the last-of the dirt and Beatrice covered it with flowers. It was a silent affair, and the saudade the two suffered was tangible in the space between them.

"Do you know why I came here as a child?"

Alex shrugged.

"This place has always been my escape." She took a deep breath and reached for a rock, running her fingers over its impossibly smooth surface. "I've always pictured a different life for myself, a different time, a foreign world. I don't fit here, at least that's how I feel—" the girl laughed nervously and squeezed the stone, "or felt. I don't know. Some fantastic tale in the woods always seemed better than what I was living. I assume that's why I like theater so much; I get to become someone totally new in a world so unlike our own."

Beatrice frowned, her eyes glued to the simple grave. Exhaling slowly, she sat the large, smooth stone over the flowers.

"Nothing's been the same since my mother died. And I think the hardest thing about dealing with her passing is seeing the pain in my father's eyes every time he looks at me." She ran her fingers through her curls and glared at the throne across the clearing. "I'm the spitting image of my mother. It's almost uncanny. As I've grown, I've realized what I have seen in his eyes is not solely a father looking at his daughter but a man seeing the face of his dead wife.

That realization hit me the hardest when I was in the hospital."

A gust of wind blew petals in the girl's face and filled her nose with the wood's lovely scent. She closed her eyes and reimagined the life her castle used to breathe into her before she lost sight of herself. The walls were tall and crisp and clean, massive windows let in the pure rays of sunlight, petals of all colors and shapes rained from the heavens to where they fell on the marble floors, and when the people danced, the flowers would create a beautiful and furious storm. Beatrice smiled to herself; she sorely missed that image. She missed the dancing. It was her mother, in fact, who had taught her to dance. They would clear the living room and practice the waltz, tango, and salsa, with her father stepping in every now and again to teach two-step.

"It's almost like I'm with her when I'm here." She was hesitant, but spoke anyway. "Her name was Lori." The girl grinned as she sat a second stone atop the first, it felt so good to say her mother's name, for it had been so long since it had graced her lips. *Lori.*

"It was my mother who gave me the courage to explore and to dream. I would have been totally different had it not been for her. Weird to think. Right?"

"Terrifying," Alex teased.

"Places like this were where she and I found comfort and where we would play for hours. The craziest thing is I think she loved it as much as I did, sometimes even more. That's just a part of me I refuse to let go. I'm strange, I get it. I've always been one of those weird, annoying kids, but it's kept me close to the memory of my mother." Beatrice traced the grooves embedded in the third stone with her thumb and frowned. The frigid air nipped at her fingers, but she refused to wear gloves. "Holding onto her like this has been so hard to bear some days. Being bullied—and, God, I *hate* that word. It sounds like I'm victimizing myself—but being bullied a little is fine. I get it. I even understood as a child. Kids can be awful. After so much of it, though, it doesn't feel like they're just a bunch of stupid kids. It feels like they simply never want you to stop suffering."

The girl added another rock to the tower of stones.

"It got so bad I had to change schools. It was after we stopped being friends, and I felt so alone, so . . . so . . ."

Alex reached for her hand and gave it a reassuring squeeze. "I—"

"Don't," she smiled and patted his hand, slipping out of his grip. "I don't blame you for anything. We all make choices." Beatrice sighed and held her hands between her legs for warmth, but as she pulled her knees to her chest, she thought maybe it wasn't for warmth but to keep herself together as she drudged up the past. "After I moved, it didn't get better. I felt more and more depressed until I eventually grew. . ." she didn't want to say it. The word haunted her, tore her apart, and would morph her into someone she hated. ". . . until I didn't want to live anymore." Beatrice shivered. It was almost as if she could feel the knife in her hand again, or the strong breeze that pushed against her as she had teetered atop the bridge that one night. "I began seeing myself as others described me. And I got into so many fights. At the time, it didn't matter who I hurt or if I got hurt myself. I didn't recognize who I was and I was only thirteen."

They didn't speak, mostly because Alex didn't know how to react.

Beatrice set yet another rock on the stack.

She was building a cairn, he realized, for Rex. His gaze traveled from the cairn to the girl. Alex had never guessed that she felt so much pain.

"What did you mean in the hospital when you said you were just trying to be happy?"

She didn't answer for quite some time. Perhaps he shouldn't have asked, Alex thought, but he didn't understand how overdosing and trying to be happy correlated.

"I found something that made me feel relaxed and, well, *free*. I don't know what happened that night and how everything got so out of control, I guess we never will, but I wasn't taking it to harm myself. I just wanted to feel happier. I didn't want to feel so insignificant."

"But you're not insignificant!" Alex wanted to scream at the top of his lungs. *Her? Insignificant?* She was one of the only things that mattered to him; a person, a soul, he would hang on to for the rest of his existence, yet she felt somehow insignificant. How had he failed her in those recent days to make her feel such a way?

"Thank you." She frowned as she placed a small stone on the cairn. "But even if you say that, it doesn't change how I feel; it's a lot deeper than that. I'm working on it, but I'm just not in a good place right now and I won't be for a while longer."

Alex nodded. It seemed to him that just yesterday their only fear was Brady Johnson and the villains they imagined in the forest.

Though, Brady Johnson had never frightened Beatrice, not in the slightest.

The two children had grown up. The little boy and girl had grown up and met the real monsters the world conjured.

"When did it all start?"

Beatrice's gaze fell on Alex. He still seemed so young, so innocent, just like the boy who used to chase after her and look at her with eyes filled with wonder when he thought she wasn't looking. That boy thought she was invincible. She was so strong and fearless and brave. And Alex knew she was audacious to a fault, but she was a marvel! As she stared at him now, Beatrice knew she had betrayed that vision he had of her.

"With Ian," she uttered.

Perhaps that's all it ever was, a vision, and she had never been anything more than a silly girl who believed she could chase away her demons with a brilliant sword that was nothing more than a stick.

"I suppose it was a little before Ian, if I'm to be honest."

"He isn't a good guy," Alex grumbled, tightening his fists at the thought of that night.

Beatrice shook her head, her eyes cast down. It's true, he wasn't a good person. Ian was mean and manipulative, but he was one of those people who showed hatred to everyone he saw except the one girl who happened to catch his attention. Beatrice was that seemingly lucky girl who basked in the affectionate attention he gave her when he was high in spirits.

"He was the first boy to ever tell me I was beautiful." Beatrice remembered that day, that very moment. She could still feel the way it made her feel when he had uttered the words, the furious beating of her heart in her chest, her skin growing hot, cheeks flushed, and the sky around them had somehow grown incredibly bright. *Beautiful,* she had thought at the time. *Me?*

Alex grimaced. She was beautiful. And though Alex had only discovered that fact five years after he first saw the girl with wild hair and bright eyes, she had always been beautiful in more ways than not. He should have told her sooner, Alex thought, he should have had the courage to tell her every day, and maybe if he had, she would have had the courage to believe in herself. Alex glanced at her, studying the frustration and sadness in Beatrice's eyes. Or maybe there was nothing he could have done.

The boy took her hand and this time she held on tight. Her hands were ice, but when asked if she wanted to head back, the girl shook her head, saying, "Not yet."

The two stared at the grave.

"I clung to him," she whispered, "and I hate that I did." She hated herself for acting so weak when all she ever dreamed of being was strong. "It wasn't that I needed him— needed anything really—but I wanted that happiness everyone else had and I truly believed that if I tried hard enough, I could find that in him. But I didn't," she chuckled, "I just ended up getting you into a fight." Beatrice exhaled slowly, squeezing his hand and relishing its warmth. "In the end, the happiness I saw in others wasn't even what I was searching for. I simply wanted something to distract myself from what I was facing."

"And what were you facing?"

Suddenly, the girl was riddled with nerves and her mouth was dry.

How could she look him in the eyes, the boy who did nothing but believe in her, and tell him that she couldn't see anything about herself that was important?

Maybe it was because of the city, or the idea that if you didn't fit the preconceived model of beauty, you wouldn't succeed. Or possibly the blame was in people in general and the hatred they planted within themselves. Or it could all have been because of her, because of her lack of strength and guts and confidence. No matter the cause, the girl was losing track of what made her worthwhile, and she had been for quite some time.

The true reason, whether the girl realized it or not, lay in the fact that as she was learning to build herself as a person, she had been torn down so many times she forgot how to stand.

Beatrice feared that no matter how many times she ran from her demons, they would always find her. All she wanted was to look in the mirror and see the young woman she had always pretended to be. Instead, Beatrice saw a woman who looked like her mother but was nothing more than a shell of a woman who didn't have the strength to accomplish anything as simple as confidence.

How could she tell him that?

She opened her mouth to speak, but silence fell from her lips.

Beatrice was weak.

She wanted to be more, needed to be more, but didn't know how. However, if Beatrice had learned anything at all from seeing the unconditional love in her father's eyes even after the accident, it was that her weakness didn't define her.

Alex sighed. She wasn't going to say anything, and he knew that. "Your weakness doesn't define you."

Beatrice smiled, inhaling and exhaling with ease as she balanced the very last stone. "You're right."

CHAPTER NINE

A meliorate

(v.) to make or become better, more bearable, or more satisfactory; improve

THE DOOR HINGES MOANED AS ALEX POKED HIS HEAD INTO the music-filled auditorium. It was pitch black save for one white light illuminating center stage. Just as she did every morning before the first bell, Beatrice bloomed under a single spotlight.

The girl danced like a surge of water, her body moving with grace and tremendous power and in perfect rhythm with all its parts.

She was exquisite in the loveliest shade of blue.

He remembered the first day blue came alive to him. Beatrice asked the boy once, so very long ago, what his favorite color was, but he had no answer. Alex never had much of a preference and never particularly cared, but when the girl guessed blue, her eyes were so bright and smile so hopeful that he told her yes. Ever since that day, blue had been a marvel.

When the music stopped, casting a thick silence over the auditorium, Beatrice remained still, holding her final pose for ages. Ever so slowly, the girl stood, rolling her shoulders and rising with the same quiet seduction as Aphrodite ascending from the foam of the sea.

"Bee," the boy's voice echoed.

She whipped around, glaring and ready to kill at the sound of her secret nickname, but she softened with a warm smile upon recognizing Alex.

Alex was a mess, he had always known it. The consistent feeling of annoyance never left him. It was as if his blood had never stopped boiling since his birth, and yet he somehow found solace in something as impeccably simple as a smile.

Her hair is as frizzy as ever, Alex thought as she approached.

As she said hello, Alex felt nervous. He gulped. "You were honest with me and if I'm to be honest with anyone, I might as well be honest with you." He frowned and dug deep into his pockets. Alex hated the desire he had to turn and walk away without another word. He hid from conflicts, and he never found the need to open up to anyone. It didn't seem like anyone really cared for his opinion, anyways, but Beatrice had never made him feel that way. With her, it was something altogether new. "I want to be different. I-I just . . ."

Alex felt stupid. *I might as well ask Beatrice for a tampon if I'm going to be so emotional,* he thought, but Beatrice wasn't the kind to judge.

She had always been so fascinating to Alex. Underneath the irritation he felt towards her and her strange ways, the boy wanted to live life the way the girl did, by diving in head first.

"I," Alex paused, "I just don't know how to do that."

Beatrice gave his arm a gentle squeeze. "Then *be* different," she grinned. "Find whatever makes you feel alive and chase that feeling every day. Within reason, of course. No drugs as an escape." She shook a finger at him and laughed nervously. Beatrice took a deep breath. "No one else matters, Alex. Whatever they say out of hatred, whatever they think about you, it just doesn't matter. All you should do is be your own person and fight for your happiness, whatever it may be. But, hey, I'm only just now relearning this myself," Beatrice winked.

THE BOY GLARED AT THE GROUND BESIDE HIS BED. IF HE KEPT enough concentration, he could almost imagine Rex at his feet.

Alex frowned as he plucked a strand of fur from his pants. Why did it have to be so hard?

His gaze fell upon the mirror where he studied his reflection. He looked sad, Alex noted, he looked skinny and sad.

Beatrice's words rang in his head.

"You've always been so serious . . . maybe later you'll be brave enough . . . you're so strong. You are . . . you've changed."

Problem was, he wasn't strong. The boy thought back to the night of Winter Formal. He traced over the scar on his face from that night. He wasn't strong at all. He had a moment of courage and that was it.

But he could change.

He could ameliorate things for both Beatrice and himself.

And the time for that was right then.

"Hey, why'd you stop reading?" Beatrice asked, poking his side.

Alex shook his head, "Oh, sorry. I hadn't noticed."

She frowned, "Everything okay?"

The boy chuckled to himself and nodded to her. He covered her face with his hand, patting her like an annoying cat early in the morning, which made her laugh as she broke free. "Yeah, I'm good. Now where was I?"

She laid on his bed, staring at the ceiling as she fiddled with his diptych sundial and he ran his fingers through her hair—or tried to, without his fingers getting caught in the curls. Alex had read that playing with a person's hair or scratching their back could make them feel better, calmer, when they're dealing with anxiety, and he just wanted to help.

The boy was reading out loud from his science books. At first the reading was dreadfully boring to her, but now it centered Beatrice. It was her therapy, lying down beside Alex and listening to him study. The closeness made her heart settle. Whenever she felt pain or anxiety creep back, she would turn on music if Alex wasn't around. She wished that was all it took, just Alex and music. The girl sighed. Beatrice went to therapy twice a week and doctor's visits had graciously been reduced to once a month.

She missed Regenald Rex terribly. The process would have been easier with him curled up beside her.

The girl looked to Alex. He wasn't paying attention to her, for he was fully immersed in a newly-released paper on string theory. Beatrice smiled. Where would she be without him?

Beatrice winced and took a deep breath. She felt terribly weak. *Don't think about it. Ignore it*, she told herself.

Alex fixed his gaze on the girl, her mass of curls seeming to fill all the space on the bed. "Are you okay?" He didn't like the look on her face.

"Yeah," she smiled, "I'm great."

He rolled his eyes. "Don't lie to me." Alex put down what he was reading and covered the girl with a blanket.

"Thank you," she whispered.

The sun was warm on her face and she felt perfectly safe under the blanket. She listened to Alex for a bit longer, breathing slowly, in harmony with his voice, and then eventually drifted to sleep.

CHAPTER TEN

Numinous
(adj.) having a strong religious or spiritual quality; indicating or suggesting the presence of divinity; mysterious or awe-inspiring

"You know, I'm a lot nicer than I used to be." Beatrice turned over the ice cream in her bowl to find the last chocolate chunk.

Alex smiled. "Why do you say that?"

"I used to never tell you when you got juice on your chin."

The boy grumbled, "I remember."

"Well, I'm telling you now. There's ice cream on your chin."

The boy frowned as she laughed, watching him fumble getting a napkin. Alex never understood how he was only a messy eater when he ate dessert.

"I think I like you a lot better with the mess on your chin."

"Of course, you do," Alex rolled his eyes, "because it makes me look like a fool."

The girl winked and took another bite.

That was perhaps her favorite part about summer, Beatrice thought: eating ice cream outside and trying to finish before it melted, and she treasured the moments most when she was with him.

"Cambridge, huh?" she muttered.

Alex nodded. In only one month he would leave for MIT. He found the concept of living so far from the only place he'd ever known strange, unsettling, and even a little terrifying.

Beatrice frowned, "You'll be so far from me."

"Have you decided where you're going yet?"

The girl let out a sigh of relief as she nodded. After months of auditions, memorizing monologue after monologue, and more rejections than she'd like to admit, she had finally succeeded. "I just found out last night. I leave in three weeks for Arizona. It's just some small theater, but—"

Alex leapt for her, nearly knocking the table over and their ice cream along with it. He hugged her so tightly that she feared she may snap in half; he had gotten much stronger in the past months.

"C-can't breathe."

"You did it!" Alex boomed as he pulled away, a great, bright grin lighting up his face."I guess I did, didn't I?"

Alex did, too, Beatrice thought as she watched him fix the table and sit down. Not only had he immediately gotten accepted to his first-choice college, but he had changed. The boy was no longer lanky, nor socially awkward. He had grown stronger in all facets of his life, and one could see the confidence in his eyes and feel his presence as soon as he walked into a room.

More ice cream dripped down his chin, but Alex caught it

instantly and took notice of Beatrice's sweet smile as he wiped the mess away. "What?"

"Nothing," she sat back in her chair. "I'm going to miss you is all."

"I'm going to miss you, too."

"You better! You better miss me a lot, and you better not forget to call me every now and then either." She pointed her spoon as if it were some deadly weapon.

Alex laughed lightly under his breath, "I will, I will! I'll even visit."

"Every month."

"You act like I'm a millionaire or something. Not every month, but I will."

"Don't you lie to me, Alex." Beatrice glared at the boy and held out her pinky.

He linked with her. "I swear."

She bit down on her thumb and said through her gritted teeth, "Bite on it."

The girl knew what this all meant, and, hell, maybe he did, too. Call and visit—it sounded so easy, so attainable, so one says it without thinking about what it means, the steadfast loyalty and commitment of it all. Yet everyone speaks the words, like the two young souls in the ice cream shop, and everyone breaks the promise. Everyone grows apart. And Beatrice understood that, but the words sure did make them feel better.

ALEX SOAKED IN THE VIEW OF HER GLIDING ACROSS THE stage. She was a storm fueling a fire, not only within him, but within the entire audience as she portrayed the calm and loving protagonist gone insane. She had a numinous beauty about her, something both frightening and fascinating, and it kept the boy on the edge of his seat.

"She's so good!" His mother squeezed his arm and grinned, turning back to the stage and watching the young girl with unmatchable pride and love.

She was good, Alex agreed with his mother, but he found her to be so much more. Beatrice was phenomenal, and the passion she displayed while on stage illuminated her.

Beatrice locked eyes with Alex. It was fast, only lasting a mere second, but in that moment, she smiled. It was a smile meant for Alex's eyes and Alex's eyes alone, and then the instant was over and she proceeded with the play, but it was a moment the boy would hold onto dearly for many years to come.

CHAPTER ELEVEN

S olipsism
(n.) belief that all reality is subjective, or that the self can know more than its own

"RUN WITH ME."

It would take a gun or a man twice his size with a clipboard and whistle threatening to fail him to get Alex to run. "No," said with a light chuckle, as if it were a joke.

"Run with me," she said so softly her words could have been mistaken for wind. "Look around you; the trees are tall, the fog has settled just right, and the world looks green. Pretend for just a moment that you're not here, that we aren't in some small forest surrounded by a dull city, but that we are in some other glorious time and it's in our blood to race through these woods." Her hands cupped his face gingerly, and he recalled his mother holding him just as dearly from some of his earliest memories. "Run with me for just this moment."

He leapt over a boulder, keeping on her heels as they

raced and discovered new lands. The hot sun beat down on the pair and the air smelled of summer, fresh and full of promise.

Fantastic birds with long, feathery tails and great, reflective beaks that seemed upturned in smiles flew beside them as Alex and Beatrice ran, passing lazy spirits lounging in the treetops. It was a bright day with no monsters lurking in the shadows. The people of King Beatrice's kingdom were out and about, celebrating the return of their king. Even the children ran alongside the pair, shouting and howling and laughing as they went.

The boy winked as he passed her, leaving the girl farther and farther behind the faster he sprinted.

"Never!" she yelled, giving Alex a gentle shove once she caught up.

Alex skid to a stop, panting and feeling incredibly out of shape.

Beatrice grinned, victory burning in her eyes, "Was I going too fast for you?"

"We've been running for ages. You can't say you're not tired. Look, your legs are shaking!"

"I will give in," she sauntered to him, raising her sword with a dangerous smirk, "when you admit I won."

He rolled his eyes. "You beat me."

"Thank you." Beatrice put her sword back in its sheath. "And you're right. I'm exhausted." Dramatically, she dropped to the ground and took deep breaths, making Alex chuckle.

Eventually, the girl stood and rested her hands on her hips as she studied the area. She did not recognize the trees, nor the dips in the ground and impossibly green grass.

"Where do you think we are?" he asked.

"I don't know."

A strange, furry creature skipped to Beatrice, sniffed her feet, and then left without so much as a word.

She grinned. "Let's explore!"

There were no people where they ventured, and no trails, either, just small, other-worldly creatures and the lingering feeling that something great awaited them.

"What do you think life is all about, Mr. Holberry?" The girl ducked under a branch, picking a flower as she went.

"I don't know." Alex glanced behind him, perhaps out of habit, to make sure that Rex passed the obstacle okay. His heart sank. Rex wasn't there. "Maybe it's just one of those questions we're never supposed to know, or there's just no meaning at all; we're just here."

Beatrice, having expected a solemn, solipsistic answer from him, nodded. "We're just here, huh?"

Alex lips curled into a small smile, "But I've come to find it as a good thing."

Suddenly, the air felt moist and water crashed in the distance.

"The river?" she pondered.

Alex shook his head *no*.

Curiosity driving Alex and Beatrice forward, they picked up their pace.

The girl squealed and ran ahead once she saw the waterfall through the breaks in the trees.

Alex smiled.

Beatrice saw fairies and nymphs, all impossibly beautiful and elegant, and they paid no attention to the two strangers. There were lotus flowers that glowed as they floated underwater, illuminating what would be a treacherous, mysterious, and dark expanse of uncharted waters.

She slipped out of her shoes and threw her sword to the side, which frightened a couple of nymphs who vanished into the trees. Beatrice stripped herself of clothing and sprinted into the waterfall's pool in her undergarments.

"Hey! Don't just dive in!" Alex called after her. "There might be things in the water!" But she had already submerged herself without a moment's hesitation.

Beatrice stayed under water for far longer than Alex was comfortable with.

He didn't trust it.

"Beatrice?"

No answer.

Grumbling, he began taking off his shoes to go in after her.

"Let's check the water before we get in," Alex muttered. "How about we make sure there's no leeches or creepy fish or water moccasins hiding? But *no*, that would be too safe, too practical. Let's just give me unnecessary anxiety. Cool."

Just as Alex stepped in, the girl rose from the water like a bullet from a gun, gasping for air.

Beatrice was like a siren, a haunting beauty in the water. The top of her breasts peeked out from the waves, her skin was wet and glistened with the reflection of the sun, her lips curled into a seductive and devious half-smile, and her eyes whispered come-and-get-me.

"What's taking you so long?" she teased, grinning. "You'll love it!"

Alex didn't waste a second wading into the water. The pool was cool and just clear enough to give him comfort from the oh-so-real possibility of some horrifying sea creature surging towards him and eating him whole.

Beatrice floated on her back, never losing her sweet smile. The sun hit the water just right, leaving the waves she made sparkling and a lovely, warm tingle on her skin. She could feel Alex close to her as he moved to lie on his back, too. A low moan seeped from his lips as he found absolute bliss.

The girl never wanted to leave.

"I think this is what life is about," she breathed in deep and exhaled slow, relaxed by the crashes of the waterfall that drummed the waves against her.

Alex stole a glance.

Beatrice exuded such peace and joy in that moment that it would appear to anyone else that she was the epitome of perfection; that she had never once felt pain, never felt alone, never once dared to question her beauty. As she floated in those moments, Alex prayed that she would stay that happy forever.

ALEX GRIMACED. DESPITE AN HOUR HAVING PASSED SINCE their swim, his socks were still wet. He hated wet socks. The boy hated a lot of things, but wet socks were one of his least favorite. Beatrice hated wet socks, too, and that's precisely why she walked barefoot, a decision that Alex had protested too many times for her to count.

"You realize how filthy that is?" he had said.

Beatrice covered her mouth with her hand and gasped, "You don't think I'll die, do you?"

"Seriously, you could get a fungus or a cut that'll surely get infected."

Alex had gone on and on, but it did not deter her.

Sometime on their long trek back, Beatrice had fashioned a crown of flowers for herself. She caressed a petal of the crown and smiled, "I feel good."

"I'm glad to hear it."

She skipped ahead of him, grinning, "I'm ready for this

next step in life!" The girl spun, arms stretched out and giddy with the idea of her bright future.

In the woods, dancing with a crown of flowers atop her head, she was a king, untouched by everything. In the end, she always had a place where she belonged: it was with the boy and the vibrant memory of Regenald as they ventured into their great unknown.

CHAPTER TWELVE

M etanoia
(n.) a profound, usually spiritual transfor-
mation; conversion of one's mind, heart, self, or
way of life

ALEX AND BEATRICE LAY ON THEIR BACKS ON THE FLOOR OF
the girl's room. It was utterly empty except for the two kids.

Beatrice frowned, wriggling on the ground. "I never liked
this carpet. It's itchy."

The boy pulled at the fibers and shrugged. "I always
wondered why you had a huge rug here while you had
carpet."

"Dad would never pay to get new carpeting," she sighed.
"I guess it doesn't make much of a difference now."

They listened to the parents talking in the other room.

A going-away party had been thrown earlier and the five
still in the house were the only ones who remained.

"Your room looks so much bigger like this."

"When it's bland and boring?" The girl felt out of place

lying on the itchy carpet in a room that had been hers, but now definitely wasn't, with no art, no lights, nothing that made her feel at home except for the light green walls she had painted herself. "You think so? It feels much smaller this way." *A little suffocating,* she thought.

Alex heard the distinct tones of his mother's laugh. "I'm not sure what my mother is going to do without you."

"Oh, don't say that," Beatrice laughed.

"No, really. She loves you."

"The real question is: what am I going to do without her cooking? Especially all the desserts."

Alex chuckled. "Starve. I know I will when I leave. Nothing is as good as hers."

"I don't know. I do make a pretty mean grilled cheese."

"I think *everyone* makes a pretty mean grilled cheese."

The girl clicked her tongue. "Oh, you sweet boy. You know so little." She groaned as she lifted herself up. "I better go check on them."

"I'll be out in a minute."

Alex lingered for longer than he probably should have. He studied the room, taking it all in with a careful eye as if not to forget a single memory.

Time moved too fast.

Beatrice moved to the kitchen where her father and Alex's parents stood.

"Enjoy your party?" David asked.

"I did. It was nice to see everyone."

Marianne strode to the girl and wrapped her in a hug that reminded Beatrice of her own mother. The girl fought back tears as she embraced the woman.

"You grew into such a wonderful, strong woman. You are going to do great things and change the world, I just know it."

"Thank you," Beatrice said as Alex's mother pulled away.

"No, thank you." David smiled. "Alex would have been so unhappy if it wasn't for you. We're very grateful."

"I'll miss you both," Beatrice said as she gave David a hug.

"Be safe out there, kiddo!"

She laughed. "I will."

"You better. No shenanigans," her father warned with a smirk.

"No shenanigans," she promised. "I, uh, I can help clean." The girl offered.

"Of course not!" Alex's mother exclaimed. "You have to get on your way!"

"I'll clean when I get back," John reassured.

"Okay, if you say so!" she sang, sprinting to the door and cackling victoriously before anyone could change their mind.

ALEX STOOD ON THE STONE PATH BETWEEN THE HOUSE AND the road with his hands deep in his pockets.

The day had moved incredibly slowly, every second lasting an hour, and it was torturous.

He was nervous about the road ahead, a feeling he couldn't shake. He looked to the house. Perhaps it was because she was leaving, because perhaps he'd never see King Beatrice again.

Shaking his head, he cast his eyes to the ground and cleared his throat. *Everything will be fine—great, as a matter of fact*, he reminded himself.

An alarming *thud* disrupted the boy's thoughts. He looked

to the house again. There she stood, though it was less standing and more of an awkward and desperate stance with a furious grip on the door handle. She was flushed, a bright grin on her face, and her chest heaved, completely out of breath.

He smiled at the girl, finding her to be so very odd.

"I thought you had left," she said once by his side.

"No, I just stepped out for a while."

They were silent, both staring at the end of Beatrice's street which seemed much farther than it had always been.

The girl fiddled with a long-lost trinket in her pocket. It was time, she furrowed her brow—time to let it all go. The knowledge burned; there's never enough time. Beatrice revealed the object. The watch was green, the color had faded slightly, but still that vibrant green she remembered when she found it sticking out from the blades of grass.

Alex's eyes grew wide. *My science watch!* His jaw dropped. The boy never thought he'd see it ever again and had forgotten about it years ago, after he received a stern lashing from his grandmother, of course. And yet, there it was: beaker, microscope, and all.

"I kept it," Beatrice whispered. "It was silly of me, but I don't know, I couldn't bring myself to give it up." She handed the watch to Alex and he took it with hesitation, as if maybe this were all a dream. He was letting go of Beatrice, so he prayed that today was nothing more than just that —a dream.

"You know what? My grandma gave me hell for losing this." Alex laughed to himself, it didn't even fit anymore. The two ends barely touched when he wrapped the watch around his wrist.

She looked at her feet. "I've put you through a lot. Haven't I?"

"I can say the same."

"No, you can't." Beatrice frowned. "I'm sorry."

"I'm sorry, too."

The two kids held each other, though they really didn't feel much like kids anymore.

They walked to the car, the parents, Alex, and Beatrice, and the last goodbyes were said to the girl as John climbed into the driver's seat.

"We'll meet you in the car," David whispered to his son as they left Alex and Beatrice on the curb.

Beatrice stared at the boy, skimming through all the memories she had with him, and as she did, Alex did the same, cementing moments with King Beatrice in which she had gifted him metanoia.

"Goodbye, Mr. Holberry. You were my greatest adventure." She smiled, but the boy saw more sorrow in that smile than joy.

Alex stood in the street long after she had disappeared around the bend, watching as if he could still see her big, bright eyes and dazzling grin emerging from her mess of curls as she watched him, too, from the car.

He still heard her voice and clung to the words without reprieve.

"And you were mine."

ABOUT THE AUTHOR

Evangeline was a hyperactive child and was forced outside to give her family a 5-minute break which helped water her already wild imagination. You can find her kayaking on the river in Austin, Tx, gazing at a bottle of White Zinfandel, or studying, but mostly keeping herself busy and in desperate need of a nap.

Keep in touch on www.evangelinebooks.com